Saturday Night Dinner

The Husband Swap: Book One

JS Gray

Spectrum Books

Contents

To all those couples who may have influenced this novel;
here's to a better, *safer* Saturday Night Dinner...

Saturday

Prologue

"Hello? HELLO...?" Shirley screamed, not caring who heard her or how crazy she might have looked to the woman walking her dog a little further down the road. Under different circumstances, Shirley may have given the nosey woman a piece of her mind, but this evening, she had something more important to worry about instead.

It was getting dark outside. Although the day had been hot, even for the height of summer, there was now a breeze to the air. It was refreshing, yet she still regretted not bothering to wrap up.

Stood on the doorstep, she had been just about to knock. The shouting had gone on long enough, and she needed an early night tonight, Saturday or not. She had the first train to catch in the morning and just had to look more presentable than her judgmental sister-in-law, who she was spending the day with.

Peering into the large bay window, its curtains not yet closed to the darkness of dusk, Shirley couldn't believe what she was seeing, yet couldn't seem to pull herself away. Her morbid fascination getting the better of her, even if was the most disturbing scene she'd ever witnessed with her own two eyes. At sixty-six, nothing had come even close, and she hoped it never would again.

Shirley knew her neighbours were the type to cause trouble, but this was something else altogether.

She'd given them an inch, and this is how they repaid her. Begrudgingly, she pulled out her mobile, adamant that they should reimburse her if any costs were occurred.

"Hello. Please help... I need an ambulance. And the police! As quickly as possible, there's blood everywhere. Yes, it's an emergency... He's been stabbed."

***

Inside the dining room, there was a strange calmness that had dampened the previous hostilities of the evening. The ticking of a clock somehow keeping rhythm to an otherwise chaotic fiasco.

The wine had been poured and the cheese, a perfectly ambient eating temperature, had been placed in the middle of the table. It was accompanied by a generous portion of grapes and celery, crusty bread and a selection of crackers, along with an array of chutneys. It had looked delicious, although no one had been in the mood to pick at it. There was no chance of that happening now, of course. The night had been well and truly ruined.

As the dark crimson blood began to seep across the previously spotless white and grey gingham tablecloth, the others knew that help couldn't possibly arrive in time to save him. For now, all they could do was to stay by his side and deal with the repercussions later.

After...

He sat there with his three best friends in just as much shock as Shirley, the nosey neighbour, was in. The night certainly hadn't been a success, but none of them could ever have imagined it would end as desperately as this. Certainly not him.

As he took another laboured breath, he felt a strange pang of sadness. Not for his own impending death, but for his remaining friends and the little boy asleep upstairs. It was such a shame that all four of their intertwined lives had changed so drastically in as little as seven days.

How could it really have come to this?

The Previous Saturday

One

"Oh my God, I can't tell you how much I've needed this drink!" James sighed to Billy as he took his first sip. "Cleo's been a nightmare all week, and I've been pulling my hair out with him. And as usual, Daniel's been as useful as a priest's ball sack."

James was the lippy one of them. Rather crass at times, but amusing with it. He rarely shut up and was the one that usually annoyed the others when he was off on one of his rants about something or other. He usually got away with it too, because he was also the ringleader, as it were, holding the others together in a nice little foursome.

James was the one that encouraged their regular get-togethers. He was also the one who had the most interesting anecdotes and, by far, the most colourful background. It didn't hurt that he was six foot four with a cracking smile, either.

"Cheers!" Billy said, ignoring the crude joke.

Without waiting for the others, he raised his glass and toasted their long-overdue evening with his best friend. Billy had been looking forward to their get together all week too. It beat staying home on a Saturday night with just his husband to talk to, anyway.

"What are you guys cheering?" Daniel asked, coming through to the dining room before following it up with a sarcastic "It can't be a hard day's work."

"Hey. I'd like to see you look after a one-year-old non-stop all week, with very little help," James replied, rolling his eyes.

Daniel had a knack for pissing off his husband when talking about their opposing roles within the family. Yet again, he was taking any chance he got to debunk what James does as legitimate 'work'. *Cheeky bastard.*

James was sure that at least half of the time he did it just to wind him up. And for the most part, it worked. If only he could ignore his husband's taunts...

"Well, if I was home playing with Cleo, or out meeting my friends for coffee every day, we wouldn't have this house to live in, would we?"

"Ooh, you didn't just say that, did you?" Billy gasped with raised eyebrows and a grin.

He enjoyed sitting back with a glass of wine in his hand, watching all the drama and the fireworks that the couple usually went through unfold. He never bickered like this with his husband, who was about as quiet as James was talkative.

Aiken finally joined the other three around the table and took a seat without a word. Like Daniel, Aiken was the main breadwinner between him and Billy. When he did have something to say, it was usually in support of his counterpart, Daniel, rather than his husband.

It was Saturday night and the four men were having dinner together. With conflicting schedules, the two couples often found it hard to get time in as a four piece. James and Billy would see each other once or twice a week at least, but with Daniel and Aiken working such long hours in order to manage their own businesses, it was hard to tie them down for a real 'couple's catch-up'.

The four of them had been friends for a long time. They were perfectly comfortable in one another's company, but it was clear that they'd stayed friends as they had because of the longevity of James and Billy's childhood friendship.

Since the group had grown that little bit older, and certainly after Cleo had come along, they had reluctantly swapped their wild nights out in the gay clubs for not-so-quiet nights in on the sofa. As long as there was a drink being served, Daniel, at least, was happy.

"Seriously, I don't know how many times I have to tell you, being the stay-at-home parent is much harder than it sounds, okay? I used to go to 'work'," he said in air quotes whilst squinting his eyes in disapproval. "I used to have a career, and I know for a fact which one is tougher. If I didn't go out and meet up with other friends and parents, I'd go stir crazy," James stressed, not for the first time. "Can you not remember when we first got Cleo? I wasn't even allowed out to see anyone for the first few months. The lack of outside contact was driving me absolutely insane."

"Well, that was just ridiculous. I can't believe Social Services would make you feel so isolated like that," Aiken complained. From what he'd heard of the 'service', he wasn't keen to deal with any of them any time soon.

"I know, as if having a new baby isn't hard enough... Then they say we've got to bond with the baby *without* seeing, or getting help from anyone else! Are you absolutely sure you want to go through with it?" James asked with a raised eyebrow.

Before Aiken had a chance to answer honestly, Billy piped up. "After what you've told us, no. But then, what other choices do we have? I mean, who knows when *I'm* going to get pregnant?" He joked with a grin before adding a little more seriously, "as long as we get a child one way or another, we don't really mind how we do it."

"Dinner should be about fifteen minutes. Anyone for a top up?" Daniel offered.

Before waiting for a response, he was making his way around the room, filling everyone's glass. Aiken hadn't even taken a sip yet, but it seemed wrong to leave him out, even if that one glass would be nursed all evening.

It was Daniel and James' turn to host this evening; it was easier for them, as it meant they didn't need to arrange a babysitter. Cleo had entertained their guests earlier. He was at that perfect age where he could walk, he could say a few jumbled words, and no matter how naughty he was, he'd be forgiven as soon as he batted his eyelashes.

Like his daddy and papa, 'Uncle' Billy had also been completely in love with Cleo with him since the first time he was able to meet him. The wait Social Services had enforced, intended to allow his new parents to bond with him properly, was almost as difficult for Billy as it had been for James. That, however, all seemed like a distant memory now that he was legally adopted and completely part of their family forever.

Billy and Aiken had arrived early to get some cuddles in. It also meant that Billy was able to help James with Cleo's bath and bedtime routine, to get that all-important 'experience' in. Cleo was now fast asleep upstairs in his cot, although Billy hadn't been able to resist popping into his room once or twice to check up on him.

The slow-roast pork belly with celeriac and pear mash was almost ready to serve up. Tonight, there was no starter, but Daniel had made a dessert, along with a hefty cheese board prepared for later. *Perfect.*

When he had the time, Daniel enjoyed creating a feast in the kitchen. But with such a busy schedule throughout the week, this usually only meant dinner on a Saturday night, or maybe a Sunday afternoon. He was usually too busy with odd jobs and other stuff around the house, as no matter how much he hinted, James never seemed to tackle them.

"Hmm. Looking forward to it. I've not had a nice home-cooked meal like this in a while," Aiken said flatly. With his dead-pan demeanour, no one quite knew if he was winding up the other half or not.

"Rude..." Billy piped up playfully, yet still wanting to stress his point. "I do work myself, you know. I might not have the high-powered business empire that you do, but I do actually go to work. And for that matter, the times I've spent with James, I can vouch for how hard it is to be a stay-at-home parent," he grinned smugly.

"Yeah, yeah. Can we change the subject? We don't want the evening to turn into a total bitch fest about how hard James works and how I don't care about anything he does," Daniel said, rolling his eyes. "I'd rather you spend it telling me how delicious dinner is, or how nice the upstairs loo looks now I've finished decorating it."

"Hey. I know. Let's talk about our sex lives. I bet you guys get it at least more than once a month, right?" James asked before patting his husband's hand. "I mean, you don't have a little kid to get in the way and you don't come in tired every night, do you, Aiken?"

"Oh. here we go again... Always whining about not getting any. Well, I do work hard and I am tired when I get in. I've got to put one hundred and ten percent in if my business is to succeed. Isn't that right, Aiken? Well, if you'd lost that extra stone or two you keep promising about, maybe, just maybe, I wouldn't be *quite* as tired." He smirked, getting his usual jab in.

James rolled his eyes. *Back on the topic of his weight again.*

It sounded horrible. The bile that was spat between one of James and Daniel's many arguments suggested that the husbands despised one another. It wasn't quite the case. It's just after being together for so long, they couldn't help but aggravate each other at the smallest of details. Unfortunately, there was some truth to Daniel's comments, both about the weight gain on James' part and the fact that if he lost it, Daniel might me more inclined to have sex with him on a more regular basis, which was something James had been asking for, for years.

But there was still love in the room. Between James and Daniel, between Billy and Aiken, and for each other. After getting to know one another so well, the bickering was just their way of letting off steam. Nothing more serious than that. The moods never lasted long, and were always forgotten ahead of their next catch up.

When they all spent time together like this, it was James and Billy that did most of the gossiping, much to their husband's irritation. Like old fish wives, they'd listen to each other moan about their husbands; what they've done to annoy them, what they've done wrong, or what they haven't done at all. It might not have been the healthiest co-dependent friendship, but at least for James and Billy, they had one another to let off steam to when their husbands weren't behaving the way they were supposed to.

"We should have just married each other instead," Billy joked to James as he blew a kiss.

"Can you imagine if we had? We'd get nothing done, and we'd be completely broke and homeless!" James laughed back.

"Yeah, you'd never get out of bed, either," Daniel added, "and who would look after us two?" He asked, nudging

Aiken, who returned the smile, just glad they were no longer bickering about how much sex they had, which was a deeply private topic he'd far rather avoid. He didn't want to be embarrassed by whatever complaint Billy might have on the subject, either.

"Let's just keep it as it is..." Aiken suggested with a sensible nod.

The subject was easily dropped when Daniel, along with the help of Aiken, served dinner. It was delicious. The smell throughout the house was perfection, and the taste of the pork didn't disappoint either. Daniel really did know how to serve up a feast fit for kings. *His one saving grace*, James would often tease.

The talk was much more light-hearted over their meal. Although the two businessmen were less interested in trivial things such as TV shows or the latest pop stars, they did both try and make an effort. However, tonight Daniel was keen to boast about Cleo now being able to recite *some* of the alphabet, although not necessarily in the right order.

"Well, if you can call 'A-B-C-B-2-S-3' the alphabet, he's a genius!" James laughed at how wonderfully entertaining his son was.

The nit-picking and cat-scratching never lasted too long and everyone was enjoying a great evening.

With three big drinkers around the table, another two bottles were enjoyed before they'd even finished their mains. It had barely touched the sides, it seemed, and at least Daniel was keen for a drop more. James' joke of him being a functioning alcoholic was probably closer to the truth than either of them would like to admit.

"I'm so sorry, guys. I don't know how this happened..." he said with an air of devastation, returning from the kitchen with a huge pavlova in his hand.

"What? What's wrong, honey?" James asked, growing a little concerned. "Have you ruined the dessert?"

"Ruined dessert? I don't *ruin* anything. I was actually rather concerned that we only have this bottle of red and then one more, and that's it," he said, genuinely disappointed.

"Oh, shit," James whispered before remembering. "Ahh, but we do have a bottle and a half of port!"

"Phew. Crisis averted. For now, at least," Aiken said, rolling his eyes, never quite understanding their addiction to the sauce.

It's not like he was against alcohol. He enjoyed a glass every now and again. It's just that he didn't see the point in drinking to excess every night. He hated having to deal with the aftermath the following morning. The rest of them were beyond teasing him about it after so many years of not keeping up with their rounds. More often than not, it usually meant he was the designated driver, so everyone was happy.

"Seriously though. I know it's hard work for you both having Cleo. But we can't wait to be parents," Billy said sincerely, taking his husband's hand. "We're so excited. So envious of you guys... Especially as you got such a young baby too. We'll never be that lucky, but I guess we could get a call for an older child any day now," he added.

"Oh God. The wait is terrible, isn't it? The social workers will never give anything away. It'll end up being a phone call out of the blue when you're least expecting it. And that's if you're lucky. It might not even happen at all."

"Oh God. Don't even say that," Billy said, deflated. "If we could just swap with you right now, we totally would."

"Ha! That would be funny, wouldn't it? A husband swap!" James said, thinking about their earlier conversation. "God, imagine how much fun me and you would have," he turned to Billy before adding, "And imagine how much money these two would make without us getting in the way of their jobs or spending every penny they made."

They all started laughing at the thought of being on that awful TV programme that aired a few years ago.

"Can you imagine how awful it would be to be filmed for twenty-four hours a day?" Daniel said, shaking his head. There was no way he'd agree to that.

"It wouldn't be too bad. That is, if they didn't mind filming me having a quick wank under the covers." James added, laughing. "Hic!"

"James, do you have to be so vulgar?" Daniel scorned, shaking his head in embarrassment.

"What? Well, I wouldn't need to if you did it for me." He grinned and blew a kiss.

Although drunk and smiling, Daniel wasn't best pleased. He hated it when James brought stuff like this up in front of other people, even it if was just Billy and Aiken. It was embarrassing, and it wasn't as if they never made love. He just wasn't as much of a sex-pest as his husband was. He was always made out to be the bad guy in the relationship, and it just wasn't fair. Plus, as he'd been clear many times, if James made more of an effort with himself and his appearance, he would be inclined to make more of an effort in the bedroom. It always fell on deaf ears, so why should he have to take all the blame?

At least Aiken would agree with him. That was if he ever got off the fence and had an actual bloody opinion about something. Chance would be a fine thing.

The others burst out laughing again, and it wasn't long before Daniel joined them. They adjourned to the living room to finish off the wine and begin the cheese. The rest of the night was fun and everyone seemed to be on top form.

They were on their last drink of the evening and James proposed a toast to swapping husbands. In fits of laughter, he had sloshed half of his drink on the rug before even raising the glass to his lips. He must have been really drunk, because that was usually Billy's signature move. The rest of them were either too polite or too drunk themselves to notice.

***

James and Daniel crashed onto the bed not long after their guests had departed. It was well after one, and James, as usual, had designs on his husband. He hoped the enjoyable evening and copious amounts of alcohol might have loosened Daniel up for some funny-business.

"Fancy a go?" he asked hopefully. He hated having to beg like this, but as the age-old saying went, 'if you don't ask, you don't get'.

"Ah, go on then, but be quick. I'm shattered," Daniel agreed rather reluctantly.

There wasn't a lot of romance to be had between the two of them these days, not after so many years together. Plus, the amount of alcohol, the lateness of the night, and the fact that Daniel just wasn't particularly into it meant that it was a bit of a struggle to even get hard.

Chancing his luck, James really wanted to top Daniel tonight. It had been at least a couple of years since his husband had let him, but tonight, with the green light, maybe he'd allow that, too. Doing his best to stay on Daniel's good side, James had worked his way down the bed to take his husband's flaccid cock in his mouth. At the same time, he was rigorously pulling on his own, trying to get stiff. But it was no good; there was no way he was up for taking the lead tonight after so many glasses of red. *It would probably have been a 'no' from Daniel anyway,* should he have tried. Not wanting to waste the offer he did have, James changed tact.

Climbing on top, he reached over for the lube and prepared himself, making sure that Daniel's dick was well oiled. It still wasn't hard, but big and firm enough to at least sit on. It should do the trick, hopefully, and James didn't mind doing all the work for a quickie.

"You ready?" Daniel mumbled as if he was going to actively do something to impress his husband instead of just lie there half asleep.

They hadn't bothered to turn the light on, but James could imagine the indifferent expression he'd be wearing. It really was a shame there wasn't a bit more passion in their love lives after nearly ten years of marriage. There used to be though, *didn't there?*

James could feel his own dick thicken a touch as he slid down onto his husband. He always found it easier to come when being fucked, even when not quite hard himself. Although he would have preferred to top for a change, a shag was still a shag.

Holding onto Daniel's arms, which were now flexed, and rather alluringly placed above his head, he began to grind. He loved feeling his husband's thickness inside of him. The sensation couldn't be beaten. It was just a shame their sex life had dried up to every couple of weeks or so, and that was only if he was lucky. He could have fooled around like this every night of the week and not got bored of it. *Who would ever get bored of being fucked by Daniel?* He was such a good-looking guy, handsome, chiselled and even had managed to keep the muscles and physique of his youth. James still wondered what he was ever doing with him.

"Fuck yeah," he moaned, now hard enough to finish off.

Bending down, he went in for a kiss.

"You like that?" he asked, pushing himself as deeply as he could into his husband's groin. "Daniel? Daniel, are you awake?" he asked. "Daniel?"

Fucking hell. He'd fallen asleep again.

As he'd started, he was resolute to finish. Grabbing hold of his cock, he furiously beat it, desperately gunning for the payoff. Grinding into his husband, it didn't take long. He had the knack down to a fine art and knew exactly what to do to get off as quickly as possible.

Determined, yet satisfied, he came over his husband's chest before sliding off Daniel's now totally soft dick. He was half tempted to leave the mess there; in retaliation, just for Daniel to clean up the following morning. It really was tempting, but he knew it would probably end up over his back anyway, should Daniel spoon him later in the night. *Chance of that would be a fine thing too.*

Reluctantly, he reached for the tissues and mopped up before falling fast asleep himself.

Across town, and Billy wasn't so lucky. He would have killed for something like that, anything really, even if Aiken had fallen asleep halfway through, but it wasn't to be this evening, just like it hadn't been for weeks or months before.

Instead, he waited until his husband was fast asleep before ever-so-gently climbing out of bed.

Thwack.

"Ouch, y' bastard," Billy cursed, in pain, as he recoiled off the chest of draws.

That was going to leave a hefty bruise on his thigh tomorrow.

With an ache in his leg to match the strain in his dick, he

crept into the spare room to jack off.

Like every other night.

The Previous Sunday

Two

Just as the group of friends had arranged to have a long drawn-out dinner with lots of wine together on Saturday night, they'd somewhat idiotically also agreed to get up early the following morning to go for a long drawn-out walk. Whoever thought that that was a good idea deserved to be ostracised from the group. James had a sneaky suspicion it might have been Aiken, who, as usual, wasn't suffering in the least.

The only saving grace was that they were heading to the pub for a hearty lunch and some hair of the dog.

Today, James and Billy were a little more hungover than usual. As the fresh air and green trees of the local woods hadn't done much to make them feel any better, they hoped that a well-deserved beer at the end of it might.

"Oh, my God, the back of my head is pounding," James groaned with a raspy voice. He cursed himself for not bringing along a bottle of water.

He was walking with Billy a few paces in front of his husband and was carrying Cleo on his shoulders. Every so often, Cleo would reach up to grab the leaves and branches above, or shout 'Doggie', which was his new favourite word. At one point he almost leapt from James' shoulders, lunging for a particularly bouncy golden retriever puppy.

"Tell me about it. I nearly threw up on the drive home. I couldn't believe how drunk you got me," Billy said, playfully nudging him with his shoulder.

"Me? It wasn't me that 'forced' that last half pint of port down your throat, was it?" James laughed in defence.

"What do you expect when you serve it in a glass like that? Alright, alright, I guess I should take *some* of the blame. Hey do you want me to take Cleo for a bit? He must be getting heavy now."

"Umm, yes please, he's super heavy and not quite back in my good books yet. Honestly, I could have strangled him this morning. He had us up, or should I say, he had *me* up three times last night crying... for absolutely no reason at all. I think he knew we were drinking last night, and he decided to have some fun of his own. Daniel isn't best pleased; I can tell you," he said, craning up to lift Cleo off his shoulders.

Cleo was quite happy to be passed over, oblivious to the trouble he'd caused.

"Bee-yee!" Cleo smiled with his hands out to be picked up. He loved his uncle Billy.

A few paces behind, Daniel and Aiken were deep in conversation.

"I can't believe how drunk James was by the time you left. As if the baby crying all night wasn't enough, there was a right mess when I'd woken up this morning as well!" Daniel complained. He looked remarkably good, considering how much he'd put back himself.

"Sorry about that. We should have stayed to help."

"No, I didn't mean that. I'm just tired. The mess was mostly where James had sat. I'm going to have to get the carpets cleaned. He can never control his alcohol and he always over does it. At least we were at home and didn't ruin anything of yours."

"Don't worry about James. Billy wasn't much better, either. I was hoping this walk would do them both some good. Instead, it just seems like they're moaning more than ever," Aiken noticed, overhearing snippets of their conversation.

"I know. I feel fine," Daniel said, on the whole, telling the truth.

"Wait until you reach forty. It's a lot harder to deal with a hangover. Believe me!" Aiken warned.

It was a struggle, but the four of them continued through the woods, with little Cleo keeping them all entertained with his banter. At least he was happy now, which was a surprise considering how awful he'd been throughout the night. How was he so awake and sprightly after such little sleep?

Cleo was totally unaware as to how rough his dad or his 'uncle' were feeling. He wouldn't stop babbling on about something or another, but at least he seemed happy. One thing less to worry about today.

Not much longer to their goal; *The Golden Lion*, and a big Sunday lunch, at least.

It would usually take hour or so to reach the pub from

where they'd parked, depending on how sprightly they were feeling, and they still had a way to go. Today had already felt like the longest morning of James' life. "I'm never drinking again!" he complained.

"Let's see if you stay dry a little longer next Saturday... we're having dinner again," Billy wagered.

"Nah, to be fair, I don't even think I'll last the day!"

Thank God Cleo was on top form today and not playing up. James didn't think he had it in him to try and deal with any tears or tantrums in his fragile state. He often joked that Cleo had reached the terrible twos early, the way he acted up when he was tired. And although he didn't mind Billy stepping in to help, it wasn't really his place to: But there'd be no chance of Daniel lifting a finger with the parenting today. He knew that for a fact. He'd stopped asking for his husband to carry, change, or deal with Cleo a long time ago. Sometimes James wondered if Daniel had ever been serious about having kids in the first place, the way he seemed to be hands-off as much as possible.

Further into the woods, and Daniel felt the need to have another word with James about his behaviour, and mess last night. Billy took the opportunity to have a quiet chat with Aiken, too.

"Hey handsome," Billy purred, trying to pull his most alluring face.

"Hey?" He replied, waiting for whatever favour, request or obscure suggestion that his husband had cooked up.

"You're not feeling bad, are you?"

"No, of course not."

"Great," Billy grinned, glad Aiken had taken the bait so readily.

"Do you fancy taking a quick detour to the *Lion*? I know a *private* shortcut."

Aiken should have known what his husband was after. He looked up at Cleo, still on Billy's shoulders, and raised an eyebrow.

"Don't worry about this little fella, hey Cleo," he said, looking up. "I was gonna pass him to his Papa, anyway. It must be Daniel's turn to take him by now."

"No thanks, all the same," Aiken said, brushing it off. "Maybe another time?"

Billy almost knew he'd be knocked back. He always was... but it still hurt. And although it was a given that Aiken wouldn't have wanted a quicky with him out in a public place like this, he had still spent the last ten minutes working up the balls to asking him, regardless: Always trying to find the best (or in this case worst) time, always judging the likelihood of Aiken agreeing or not. Unfortunately, nowadays it was almost always a 'not now, maybe later' stock response. For some reason, later never came.

Disappointed but unsurprised, Billy caught up with James, allowing Daniel to fall back into conversation with his rather boring husband.

Hangovers aside, it was a lovely day to be outside for a walk. The sun was shining, the birds and the butterflies were out and everyone they passed greeted them with smiles and 'hellos'. Daniel had stopped to chat to a customer at one point and Billy had tried to avoid a guy he'd had a rather unfortunate date with many moons ago but all in all, the group was in good spirit by the time they'd finally reached the end of their walk. The five of them all piled in to the pub. James, Billy and Cleo went to find a table as Aiken and Daniel made their way over to the bar to take care of business, just as they did every time they were out together.

The olde-worlde, traditional English country pub was relatively quiet for a sunny Sunday afternoon, but it was sure to pick up over the next couple of hours. *The Golden Lion* always did, being such a popular pub with a reputation for great, homely food.

Before the rest of them had even settled, Daniel and Aiken had already joined them, armed with drinks and menus.

"I'm starving," James admitted, rubbing his grumbling belly.

Rolling his eyes, Daniel replied, "you're always starving!"

"What? We've walked for miles. I didn't have much of a breakfast."

"I must admit, I am pretty hungry myself now. Think I'll have the steak and ale pie. With some chips," Aiken agreed, trying to defuse another spat between the pair.

"Good. Let's get some fat on those bones. More of you to love, honey," Billy joked, grabbing his husband's waist. "Would you look at this... No love handles. What am I supposed to swing from?"

"Shhusssh," Aiken pushed his husband's hands away,

blushing. "The rest of the pub doesn't want to hear you talk like that, and neither does Cleo." As usual, he was completely embarrassed by his husband's brashness.

"You can't take him anywhere," Daniel added, whilst making his mind up. "I'm going to go for the all-day breakfast."

"I'm going to... go to the loo. Can you get me the full roast, please?" James asked as he left the table.

It was much busier around the other side of the bar, the bit that didn't serve food. There was some sporting match or other on, and quite a few punters presumably on their third or fourth beers already, judging by the loudness of their cheering.

By the time he'd finished in the gents, there was a sizeable crowd forming at the bar too, so he had to weave in and out of people just to get back.

"Alright, Mate," James heard, coming from one of the tables.

"Oh hey, how's it going?" he asked, with a broadening smile.

It was Duncan, Daniel's one and only employee. Rather young, but incredibly handsome, none the less. It could have been him up there on the TV, playing in the premier league, thought James, desperately trying to stop his eyes from wandering down Duncan's muscular legs, which were on display in a pair of incredibly tight fitting shorts.

"Not bad, thanks. You got a day off from the little one to watch the footie?"

"Na, they're through there. I'm with Daniel, if you want to

say hi?"

"You're alright mate," Duncan laughed. "I see enough of him at work! Tell him I said hi though."

With that, Duncan was back to the match, cheering along with his table of friend.

There were a couple of other faces dotted about that James recognised, but no one he'd know the name of. He hadn't realised how loud the bar had got in there until he'd left and made his way back into the restaurant.

On his return, James had passed the message on just as Daniel had got up to get another round in. Nosily wondering who Duncan was with, Daniel was tempted to go and say hi himself, however there was no time for that now as their food was already being served.

They were all impressed at how quickly their order came out regardless of how quiet it was in the restaurant, and wasted no time in tucking in to their meals.

"So then, gents, when are we going to do the swap?" Daniel asked out of the blue.

Just about to put a forkful of beef in his mouth, James paused. Slightly confused, he asked, "what swap?"

"The husband swap you were so keen on last night. Billy seemed well up for it, too, if I remember rightly."

"I didn't mean it exactly like that. I meant... ah well, anyway, I was obviously joking," he shrugged.

"Joking aside. After such a terrible night with the kid, a week away from the mad-house would *really* help me get some work done. I've got a couple of big orders to fulfil this week and I know I'm going to struggle, particularly if Cleo keeps me awake one more night," Daniel admitted without reluctance.

"Hey. Are you trying to bail on me already? It's not like you do anything during the night, anyway. It's always muggins here that gets up to see to him," James grunted, rather annoyed.

"Are you being serious? You think I slept at all last night? Three times he woke up crying. Three times he *woke me up* with his crying. I counted them. Three!" he said, holding his fingers up. "I've barely had any sleep at all, and *I'm* the one that has to go to work the following morning. You can lounge around as long as you want to..."

"Well, you're welcome to crash at ours for a week, Daniel, if you need a decent night's sleep. It would get Billy out of my hair, and maybe we can have an adult conversation for once, rather than talking video games and Ariana Grande all week?" Aiken suggested with a shrug.

James and Billy first looked at their husbands, and then their best friend's husbands. All four of them considered it for a moment, and with nervous smiles, agreed to a week's peace and quiet from one another.

"Looks like I'm moving in with you then!" Billy said with a grin, raising his glass to his new 'husband'. For the week, at least...

James thought it would be fun to have Billy staying over for a few days. Instead of Daniel complaining that the washing hadn't been done, or the vacuuming wasn't thorough enough, he'd get to stay up late, drink too much and eat loads of junk food, *without the nagging about his 'ever expanding' waistline*. Maybe he and Billy could even take up a new hobby together. He always wanted to try tennis, but it was pointless playing against Daniel, who was clearly far superior in anything to do with sport or fitness than James had ever been.

Daniel loved his husband, but a few days' rest bite whilst he had so much to do at work would be a godsend. He'd barely be at Aiken's house anyway, as he was already planning long days and late nights at the workshop. But knowing he wouldn't be returning to a crying baby (which he meant just as much about James as he did Cleo) or a mess in the kitchen was enough to convince him that staying with Aiken for the week was a fantastic idea.

The five of them hungrily finished off their meals before reluctantly leaving the pub for the slow trek back to their cars. At least they'd get to burn off a few of the extra calories. Making plans to move back to their respective homes when they regroup for dinner next Saturday, they all seemed to be looking forward to their rather unusual week ahead.

True to form, not ten minutes in, Billy—overexcited as usual, was jumping about and showing off for Cleo. Before he knew what was happening, he'd stumbled off the main path, fallen down the shallow bank and had ended up with his bottom in the stream that meandered its way alongside their path. However, even a wet, muddy arse couldn't stop him from being in a good mood, not now he had a week of fun with his best friend to look forward to.

As they discussed their swap, there were a few ground rules that were covered, obviously in jest, rather than any actual concerns about impropriety.

James had to promise he wouldn't get rat-arsed each night. Daniel found this impossible to believe, knowing exactly how bad and influence Billy could be on him. Aiken was just as concerned about the prospects of his husband sleeping in late for work, or even missing it entirely. Reluctantly, both James and Billy agreed this was a wise decision.

"You'll have to keep Cleo all week, though, James," Daniel was quick to add.

It was a given, anyway, as the logistics of swapping him back and forth wouldn't be worth it. Quite frankly, Daniel wouldn't know what to do with Cleo for a week by himself, and they all knew it. So, childless and husbandless, Daniel was going to rather enjoy the extended break.

"Fine. No shagging for you two though..." James joked, before all of them bursting out laughing.

"Can you imagine?" laughed Billy. "No chance of that with their sex drives!"

"Fine. None for you either. And that also means no hanky-panky with yourself, either!" Daniel said to Billy with a grin... "I've heard the rumours about how much Kleenex you get through."

"How am I gonna...? Never mind." Billy said, not quite sure it was a good idea to try and defend himself regarding his private hobbies.

They all knew that they all did it, but to talk about doing it when your friend was sleeping in the other room might have been a little bit too much. Maybe he actually would have to give it up for the week.

"Hey Cleo, do you want Uncle Billy to move in for the week?"

"Yeah yeah! Uncle Bee Yee."

Billy had an extra day or two booked off this coming week anyway, so what better way to spend them with his best friend and his favourite little guy?

The week ahead was going to be great fun!

***

James had barely remembered the conversations from last night, and although the suggestion was strange, it certainly had its upsides. Mostly, it would be a relaxing, fun week in which he'd probably get more help with Cleo than he'd ever had before whilst Daniel had been around.

Daniel also knew that being away from James had many advantages. There would be no nagging about what time he'd be returning home, if he'd make it in time for dinner, or even to see Cleo off to bed. He'd be able to leave without being told he's 'Waking the whole house up'. He was pretty sure he wouldn't have Aiken checking up on him, or his comings and goings. A key, and a spare bedroom hopefully meant that Aiken wouldn't even know what he was up to half the time. After all, he'd warned him that he'd be in his workshop most of the week. With a genuine smile, he started to think this might turn out to be the best idea they'd all had in a very long time.

Billy, like James, was looking forward to having a bit of fun. Letting his hair down and just being able to relax without Aiken fussing about the kitchen being messy, or him staying in bed too long. Aiken might complain far less than Daniel, but that didn't mean he was the easiest going of housemates. More often than not, it was just a look he threw Billy's way that told Billy he'd done something wrong.

Aiken, although keeping quiet about it, was the only one of the four of them that was reluctant to go through with it. More than anything, he would miss seeing his husband on a daily basis, or falling asleep with him each night, even if he'd never admit it aloud.

***

They had finally made it back to the cars, just about in one piece by the time the heavens had opened. If they were quick, they might just manage to stay relatively dry.

James was trying to strap Cleo in without waking him whilst Daniel sat in the driver's seat, grumbling impatiently.

They said their goodbyes, and with a warning from Aiken not to get mud everywhere, Billy's phone beeped.

Sorry havent been in touch for a while. RU free 2 meet tomoz? I could come to CU. Excited so I didn't want to w8 any longer. Dx.

Fucking hell. I wasn't expecting this so quickly, Billy thought as he read the message.

His hands were even shaking from the excitement of it all. Shielding the screen from Aiken, he felt terrible for hiding something like this. But there was no need for his husband to find out about any of it. Not until he was sure, at least.

He'd now realised that there were even more advantages to staying with James other than just pigging out, binging and having a load of fun with Cleo. His first in-real-life meeting.

Perfect!

Maybe he could pop out. A quiet café or the park somewhere. Or would they need more privacy than that? He could ask James for some space tomorrow, borrowing the house for himself for an hour or two. James wouldn't mind if Billy had someone over, *would he?*

He wouldn't get all funny about it, asking random questions or ruining it. Billy thought that James might want to stay. Help out, get involved somehow?

Billy's first 'introduction', if you could even call it that, was going to be a rather anxious and awkward affair anyway... Having James there would probably ease his nerves slightly.

He quickly text back, giving the address and suggesting a time.

The week ahead was shaping up to be even more interesting than he'd imagined.

Three

With everything happening so quickly, James really needed to pop out and get a few 'essential' supplies from the supermarket. He could have probably avoided the Co-Op for another day or two, but with Billy and his legendary appetite on the way, James took the opportunity to stock up accordingly. It's not like he minded extra snacks and treats in the house, either. He had taken Cleo and left his husband behind to pack in the peace and quiet of an empty house.

"C'mon Cleo, are you going to be a good boy for Daddy?" he asked, trying to gently wake his son.

"Dadaa. Whadabbaa." He smiled, grabbing out for James' face.

Ouch... Another day, another finger in the eye.

Giving him a quick kiss on the head, James pulled him out of the car seat and carried him over to the trolly. He'd have to be quick, as Cleo would be crying for his tea before long and he didn't usually like to wait. James tried to stick to as rigid a routine as possible, but every now and again, he didn't mind making an exception.

It was so much easier now Cleo was a little older, even if he was getting heavier and more difficult to keep in the trolley. Cleo would sit up and enjoy going shopping. He loved seeing people and looking at all the bright colours and weird and wonderful shapes in the supermarket. It was a good way of teaching him things, too. James made a point of picking things up to tell Cleo what they were. It beat looking at those monotonous flashcards he'd already gone through a hundred times, that was for sure.

Cleo had recently started walking, but taking after his less than energetic daddy, he preferred to be carried around whenever possible. Who could blame him?

"Now Cleo. I don't want you telling Papa about this. I'll be in lots of trouble if he finds out what we've been buying and you don't want that, do you? This has to be our little secret, okay? Ours and Uncle Billy's."

"Bee-yee." He grinned cheerfully.

"That's right. Uncle Billy is coming to stay with us."

James really didn't want to take too long today. In and out and be back home before Daniel left for the week. Knowing him, Daniel could pack and leave for a month without thinking about saying goodbye to either of them. Although James was looking forward to the change of pace, not catching Daniel in time would have been unthinkable.

Rushing, James had already made a list of the few things he needed, although he knew it was inevitable that other items would find their way in there too. In fact, it was fair to say that he'd probably end up with a trolly full of junk food instead.

Making good progress, they had quickly managed to make it halfway around the store in record time. Up and down the aisles Cleo had actually proved to be very entertaining. That was until he had pointed and laughed at the old man with a plastic bag on his head. With its edges folded back on itself neatly, it almost looked like a hat. *Almost.* James could have forgiven him, if it had actually been raining. Fortunately, the crazy guy hadn't noticed Cleo staring, and had wandered off muttering to himself, leaving the vague stench of urine in his wake. *You wouldn't get that in Waitrose.*

With plans never to shop at this particular Co-Op again, James left the crisps behind in favour of much needed alcohol. Moments later, he had a bottle of champagne in one hand and a bottle of prosecco in the other, weighing up the pros and cons.

"Who are we kidding?" he asked Cleo, putting the Champagne back and swapping it for a second prosecco.

"Well, hello hello, stranger," he heard from behind.

That voice... Where do I know that voice from?

With a bizarre sense of foreboding, James turned around apprehensively, not sure he was ready to deal with the consequences.

Oh fuck.

"Kirk... What are you doing here?" he asked without even pretending to be pleased to see his ex-boyfriend.

"Charming, Jamie. You haven't seen me in over ten years, and this is how you greet me."

Standing back a little, Kirk looked him over from head to

toe. He wasn't even hiding the fact he was giving James the once over. It made James' skin crawl. As if he needed Kirk's approval after everything that had happened.

"What do you want Kirk?" he asked, before giving his ex the opportunity to say something offensive about getting older, fatter, or ever so slightly balder.

"I only said hello!" he said, feigning offence.

"Well, what do you expect after how you left things? Are you here just to cause trouble again?"

"Calm down Jamie. I'm just saying hello. I've not come over to start a fight, or cause trouble."

Ugh. Kirk was the only person that ever called him Jamie. He'd not really liked it back then, but after everything that transpired between them, he'd grown to downright hate it now.

"I thought you were still in Jersey, anyway?" James said, not buying a single word Kirk was saying. He was always a bit of a slippery one that couldn't quite be trusted, even at the best of times.

"I was, but I'm back home now. For good this time. How exciting, right? I can't wait to catch up with you properly. I'd love to see Billy and Daniel, too. How is Daniel, by the way? You're still together, right?" He smiled before finally looking down into James' trolly. "Oh, my God. Who's this gorgeous little man? Is he yours? Well, that explains why you've let yourself go." James must have pulled a face because he quickly added, "You know... the baby weight," as if James had given birth himself.

James saw right through it. Amongst many of his reckless, selfish acts, Kirk had nearly derailed his and Daniel's wedding. There was no way he would be inviting him over any time soon. Daniel had always got on well with him, though, unfortunately, so there was definitely an element of having to tread lightly. He could almost imagine Daniel meeting up with him just to spite James for some recent spat or other, and that would be far too dangerous a thing to let happen.

"Yes, Cleo is mine," he said, before curtly adding, "and Daniel's, of course."

If Kirk wasn't going to take the hint in a minute, James wouldn't be able to stop himself from giving him a piece of his mind. Or, he'd be halfway out of the shop, having walked off mid conversation, no matter how rude.

"Well, hello Cleo," he said, bending over. "Aren't you a cutie? You obviously take after your handsome daddies."

"Ceeeooo," the toddler grinned, poking his fingers out again.

Shame he didn't poke Kirk's eye's clean out.

"We've got to go," James said, yanking the trolly from under Kirk's nose.

"Yikes, look at the time! I must dash! How about Saturday for drinks?"

"Can't. We have friends over for dinner."

James wondered if he'd be brash enough to try and wangle an invite. The look on Kirk's face suggested he was seriously considering it.

"Well, if you can't do Saturday, I'll look forward to having that drink with you all very soon. Maybe next weekend instead? I won't take no for an answer. Nice to see you!" he shouted, walking off in the opposite direction.

For fuck's sake.

As if James didn't have enough to think about this week with Daniel being away, now there was his meddling ex's return to deal with too.

He did his best to get back into the swing of shopping. There were a few more bits he wanted for the week, one or two more treats. Strangely, he'd somewhat lost his appetite after that not-so-welcome blast from the past. Still in a bit of a fluster, he instead opted to pick up some more alcohol and call it a job done.

Best get back to his husband before it was too late.

***

Well, that was a nice surprise. Unexpected, but nice.

Kirk hadn't banked on bumping into James in the Co-Op. He'd certainly counted on seeing him before too long, just not so soon after returning. That little impromptu encounter was a pleasant surprise that could even work in his favour, if he played things right.

Unfortunately, Jersey hadn't panned out quite as he'd expected it to. In fact, it had gone much worse. He'd left quite abruptly, and there was no way he was going to be able to go back to the island in a hurry. He had wanted to stay, of course, but after what had happened, his only option was to leave as quickly and quietly as possible to avoid any more trouble.

Every cloud had a silver lining, and his was waiting for him on his return it seemed.

Clearly, James hadn't been pleased to see Kirk. Under the circumstances, that wasn't a surprise. They had parted on bad terms, and there was a lot of ground to cover, but in the end, Kirk was sure he'd get what he wanted.

He usually did.

Four

"I can't believe we're actually doing this," Billy said to James. He had a loaded bag over his shoulder and a big smile on his face.

"I know! I seriously thought we were only joking last night, but Daniel seemed very keen about it this afternoon... although to be fair, he was pretty pissed off about having such a shitty night's sleep, so I can't really blame him."

James helped Billy with his bag, took his coat and hung it up before adding, "but if you're getting freaked out about it, or you think you're gonna miss Aiken too much we don't actually have to go through with it, I mean, it was kinda silly for us all to do this. Better still... you can keep Daniel for a week and then I'll *really* get a break."

"Freaked out? Why would I be freaked out? It'll be fun. We'll have a blast, and you know that I'll *actually* help you with Cleo."

"Ahhh, music to my ears!"

"Where is he, anyway?"

"Already in bed. Now, I know we promised we wouldn't, but do you fancy a little drinkipoos, you know... to celebrate your arrival properly?"

Billy looked deadpan at his best friend. "Do you actually need me to respond, or was that a rhetorical question?"

"Of course I don't need a response. I was gonna pour you one, anyway. We really should make the most of this week, shouldn't we? After all, we deserve it. Have you eaten yet?"

It was nearly eight o'clock by the time Billy had arrived. There were a few bits he needed to do at home, tidying around and sorting out some clothes for Aiken. And obviously, he needed to pack. Billy being Billy, he had definitely taken far longer than he should have, not that it mattered to James at all.

James and Cleo had returned from shopping just in time to say goodbye to Papa. With a stack of dog-eared paperwork under his arm, and clothes and other bits and pieces packed into his large holdall in his other hand, they saw him off on the front doorstep. It was quite emotional, for James, at least. He'd not been without his husband for an entire week like this in years. Cleo would be none the wiser, no doubt, but James would definitely struggle with his partner's absence. Daniel, of course, showed little emotion as he kissed his husband on the cheek. Sometimes James wondered if his husband acted like this just to frustrate him or if it was because he just didn't love him as much.

Somehow, though, between them, it all seemed to work out quite well in the end. With minimal fuss or drama, Daniel and Billy had swapped homes for the week as simple as that.

"I've not eaten yet, no and I'm bloody starving!" he said, rubbing his soft belly.

"How's stuffed pasta for you? I would have got something nicer in, but it was all kinda last minute, after actually forgetting about our plan last night. Well, it's not even that I forgot so much in that I didn't think we were actually being serious!" he laughed. "I did manage to nip out earlier, but I ended up running into... err, running *out of* time."

He really didn't want to think about Kirk, let alone bring him up in conversation. He knew Billy would know what to do about it, but for tonight at least, he didn't want to spoil their fun by going into any of the details. He hated thinking about that knob head, and until recently, he'd done a pretty good job of blocking him out of his mind completely. What were the chances of bumping into him like that today in the supermarket after ten years?

"Pasta's fine."

"Great, I'll stick it on the hob and open a bottle. I bought some garlic bread too. Go make yourself comfortable. Oh, and I've made up the spare bedroom for you. Get yourself all settled in."

"You mean we're not going the whole hog and you *don't* want to share a bed with me then?" Billy joked playfully. "Yeah, I'll just go and drop my bag off, and hang up a few bits. How do you think the husbands are doing?"

"They'll be fine, sensible pair they are. I can't imagine they'll be having much fun this week, though," James laughed, knowing that neither one of them were known for their exciting personalities or ability to have fun.

***

"Cheers!"

"Cheers. Thanks for having me," Daniel said with a questionable smile.

After all, out of the foursome, it was Daniel and Aiken that were the furthest removed from one another. There was no particular reason, it's just they weren't best friends. And as they weren't married to one another either, they just didn't have that much of a connection. As far as Daniel was concerned, Aiken was a hard one to crack at the best of times, with him being so reserved.

The foursome got on fine, but it was well known that they were so close only because of James and Billy's longstanding and unbreakable friendship.

"No problem, you know you're welcome anytime. Do you think you'll last a full week without James, though?"

Does this man not know me at all? thought Daniel.

"Ah, yes, I think I'll survive." He grinned. *In fact, I've really been looking forward to the break.*

"And without Cleo?"

"That'll be harder. But even if I was home, my early mornings and late nights would have meant I wouldn't get to see much of him, anyway. Speaking of which, are you sure my coming and going won't disrupt you too much? James is always complaining that I'm waking him up with my early mornings."

"Its fine, honestly. I have pretty long days, usually myself. I'm a deep sleeper, so I probably won't even hear you," he lied, not quite knowing why. "Not a problem at all. Do you reckon they'll get up to any mischief?" Aiken pondered, with the fainted hint of concern in his voice.

"I'm expecting it. I'm just glad I'm not there to have to clean it up."

"Me too!" he said, clinking glasses again. "Here's to a peaceful, quiet week without our 'better halves'!"

They were sitting in Aiken's lounge. It was so much smarter and far more tasteful than Daniel's. There was no crayon work on the coffee tables, no torn and tatty books on the shelf. The corners of the room weren't filled with Duplo or other toddler toys. No stains on the couch, or lingering smells, the list just went on and on. It was refreshingly mature and so tranquil. Daniel could really get used to this.

Obviously, he loved James and Cleo, but it was all a bit much sometimes. The shouting and screaming; the mess... and that was mostly just James. Cleo's stinky nappies didn't help, but at least James was the one to deal with that side of business. Yes, he was really going to enjoy himself this week. It was just a shame that he had to get up so early tomorrow morning.

***

"Another?" James offered cheekily.

"Go on then. Why not, eh? I don't have work tomorrow, so it's not like I have to be up early. As long as you're sure I'm not keeping you up?"

"HA! Definitely not," James laughed, going to fetch another bottle of wine from the kitchen.

They both knew that their husbands wouldn't expect them to keep their promise of sensible alcohol-free evenings all week, anyway. They didn't stand a chance: After all, it was well known that they were bad influences on each other.

With Daniel nagging so frequently about him 'not working' he may as well make the most of it whilst he could. Sure, he'd have to deal with Cleo when he woke up, he could do that on autopilot even with a monster hangover. He'd had enough practice, that was for sure.

"Should we do something this week?" James asked as he returned with the wine and a big packet of sour cheese pretzels.

"Like what? You mean go on a date?" Billy laughed.

The second joke of the evening about them two shacking up didn't go unnoticed by James. *How loved-starved was he?*

"Not a date, you sod. I mean something with Cleo. Maybe the zoo. Or take him to the beach, if you've got the time?"

"I'm off tomorrow, all day Wednesday and on Saturday, too. We can do whatever you like. Oh my God, these are amazing!" Billy said, helping himself to more pretzels.

"I know, right? Daniel's always pulling me up for buying 'crap' to eat. He acts like he doesn't snack on anything, but I know he does when he's at work. I've seen the wrappers in his bin," he explained rather defensively. He failed to add the obvious: That Daniel goes to the gym regular and has a beach-body, whereas James goes to the fridge regularly and has a couch-body.

"Maybe he's got another fella in there. Another James at work. Can you imagine it!" Billy howled.

"Lucky him. That would explain why he's never interested in me!"

"He's only mucking about. Aiken is the same when it comes to our sex life. At least you two still have sex."

"Maybe. That doesn't mean it doesn't get me down sometimes. He's constantly referring to my weight. Yeah, I might have put on a bit extra since we met, but who can seriously fit in the same clothes they could when they were twenty?"

"Aiken can," Billy said, rolling his eyes. "It's ridiculous. He can be the same as Daniel sometimes, to be fair. A couple of comments here and there about me being 'lazy'. Just because he exercises occasionally and literally hasn't put a pound on since I've met him, he thinks it's weird that I couldn't stay the same."

"I mean, come on..." James said, "look at us both. Yeah, we've filled out a little, but it's not like either of us is *huge*."

"Well, speak for yourself... I think my body type is now officially teddy bear," Billy said grimly, before smiling and grabbing hold of his midriff to jiggle it about.

He'd got used to making a joke about his weight. It somehow stopped people giving him that pity stare: the one that suggested he couldn't help it and that the world was being so cruel to him. He joked to avoid shit like that, but it didn't mean he wasn't a little self-conscious about it. In fact, James was the only person he did feel relaxed around when it came to his size.

"Yeah, but you *do* look okay with it. I mean, it suits you. You'd just look odd if you were super skinny."

"Hah. I've never been skinny, as you well know. No chance starting now, either. I would love it if Aiken could put a stone or two on, though. He'd look great a bit fuller. Don't get me wrong, I still fancy the pants off him... *Or I would if he was ever in the mood*, but with him now being forty, I think he'd look even better just a little bit *thicker*. You know, fill out one or two of those stress-wrinkles he's getting on his forehead. Yeah, he'd definitely look better a touch heavier. I mean, look what happened to you!"

"Hey, I thought you were on my side," James squawked.

"I am! Without a doubt you look far better now than when you were that skinny little twink with the awful asymmetrical haircut," he laughed, thinking back to James' early noughties 'style'. To be fair, his wasn't much better, but he was keen to keep quiet about that.

"Please don't remind me... but thanks."

"And it's not like I'm that much bigger than you, am I? You know what I reckon it is... I think it's just excuses. They're past it. They're no longer interested in sex, and are looking for excuses to 'let us down gently', so they don't have to admit they can't get it up anymore." Billy said scowling, as though he might be on to something.

"You think them calling us fat is gentle?" James asked, wondering if it could be true in some twisted way.

"Well, as far as I'm concerned, we both look pretty normal. We haven't changed that much since meeting them, and whatever they say, we definitely aren't huge."

"Agreed!" James said, raising his glass again, remembering how good his best friend was at cheering him up and lightening the mood.

Heaven help them both if he was right. If Daniel and Aiken really were past it, would that mean they'd never really be interested in sex again?

***

Daniel woke up in the middle of the night. His mind was racing after such an explicit dream. With a rock-hard boner, he was lucky he hadn't already cum over the sheets, he was so turned on. It was so vivid and *exciting*. He rarely dreamt, or remembered his dreams, at least, but just now he was really going for it. Fucking with the energy of his twenties. And it felt all the more exciting that in his dream he wasn't fucking his husband, either.

For the first time in weeks, he was actually in the mood to fool around with James. Reaching over to his husband's side of the bed, he remembered that James wasn't there. A moment later and then he realised where he was, and what he was doing in Aiken's spare room. His dick was awake and ready to go, but with no one to use it on, it would have to be wasted.

Maybe this week would be harder than he was expecting, or maybe he'd just have to occupy himself in other ways.

***

Aiken hadn't slept. He had a lot on his mind at the best of times, but tonight felt much worse. Although he probably wouldn't admit it aloud, he was missing Billy. Warm, cuddly, fluffy Billy, who sex-drive aside, he loved with all his heart.

Aiken didn't really know why he found it hard to show his affection, but he always had. It wasn't easy to say 'I love you', even to his husband. It wasn't easy for him to wrap his arms around Billy and show him he cared. But he really did care, and he really was missing him.

It felt like he was without an arm, not having Billy wrapped around him in bed like he was used to. Aiken shouldn't have let James bring up the swap again today. He could have changed the subject or told them they were all just drunk last night. He should have kept his mouth shut, like he always did, and not suggest so readily that Daniel was welcome to stay over. At the time, he hadn't really thought of the ramifications, or what it would mean for him to lose Billy for seven whole days.

Aiken was more than happy to host Daniel for as long as he wanted to stay, but that didn't mean he wanted Billy out of the picture in exchange. He wouldn't admit it to anyone, but this week with his husband sleeping away was going to be much harder than he thought.

***

James was finding it hard to get to sleep.

Seeing Kirk out of the blue like that had really thrown him for six. James had long thought that that part of his life, and Kirk in particular, were gone for good; never to be revisited, reopened, or reassessed again. Seeing him brought back difficult memories of James being a different person; young, childish, and selfish. More than anything, James couldn't stand being reminded of who he was back then. That's all Kirk was to him, a bitter reminder that James was once a selfish prick who wasn't worthy of a happy life with a handsome husband and a beautiful son.

If Kirk had any designs on rekindling anything with James, he was sorely mistaken.

As if thinking about his ex-boyfriend wasn't bad enough, what was really keeping James awake was the fact he was already missing the warmth of his husband. A soppy bugger at heart, even with Daniel spending most nights rolling away or pushing James off, he still missed having him there.

It saddened him a little to imagine Daniel, probably having the best night's sleep of his life, without a thought about missing him.

Was Billy missing Aiken in the same way?

***

In the next room, Billy was also finding it hard, quite literally, to drift off. He had a raging boner which he knew would prevent him from getting to sleep. Usually, he would have gone into the spare room to quickly toss one off, but tonight was quite different, and there would be a raised eyebrow or two if James had walked in on him doing that this evening.

Even though he had the bed and the room to himself, he felt too weird about doing it tonight. Almost as though somehow, he'd get caught having a wank in James' house. He didn't even want to imagine how awkward that would be.

There was one time at university when he'd drunkenly shagged a guy in James' university dorms. It was fine at the time; they were all young, free and single, and shagging about whenever and wherever they could whilst being students. Well, James had been, at least. Billy, on the other hand, was very reserved back then, only having a couple of relationships and the number of one-night stands could be counted on one hand... Shagging a random guy at James' was a mistake he'd never repeated.

But this was different. Now they were grown-ups and married. It felt perverse somehow to be even thinking about having a wank, or even his own dick whilst sleeping at his best friend's house.

No. He wouldn't do it. He couldn't. It would be wrong.

Billy briefly wondered if James and Daniel would have had sex together with him sleeping over, if they were both there together, that was.

By all accounts, they don't have much sex, anyway.

I wonder if James would have a wank in his own bed this week?

Billy knew that James masturbated a fair bit, too. He often complained about his husband's lack of interest, saying he needed it to 'release tension' somehow. Was that just a bit of playful banter, or was there some seriousness behind James' frustrated remarks over the years? From what Billy knew, there probably would be, so it seemed that both James and Billy suffered from the same problem, in that respect. So much about gay guys not being able to keep it in their pants, constantly shagging all the time... if only that were true!

Uh oh, it's weird thinking about James or his cock. He's like a brother, well, almost. Plus, it's not helping my own boner go down.

Billy didn't know if he could last all week without any action, even if it was only with himself.

It was going to prove tough getting to sleep tonight.

The Previous Monday

Five

Surprisingly, James had slept extremely well by himself. If he was honest, he'd probably admit that it was the best night's sleep he'd had in a long time. Although he hadn't wanted to be alone, he couldn't argue that having the bed to himself had been amazing. There was no heat radiating from his 'always-running-on-hot' husband, and having the full extent of the mattress to stretch out on meant he could toss and turn all night long without being moaned at or shaken awake by a rather grumpy Daniel.

What's more, after he woke at five to give Cleo some milk, they were both able to go back to sleep for a few hours without Papa distracting them at whatever ungodly hour he decided to get up for the day. *Thank God for having a lazy baby.*

James finally stirred again at eight fifteen. Not wanting to wake Cleo, he quietly crept downstairs, one tip-toed step at a time. After putting the kettle on, he was keen to chance his luck at having an uninterrupted shower.

The house was deadly silent save for the ticking of the grandfather clock in the hall. He wasn't used to the peace and serenity, but was enjoying it none the less.

Back upstairs, as gently as he could, he pulled the stiff shower door open. After a bit of heave-ho, he yanked it open and reminding himself to get it fixed. It was new and still sticking a bit after Daniel had finished the renovations.

He cranked the shower up as far as he could take it. The hot water was bliss on his skin. Both relaxing and purifying, he stood under the boiling heat and enjoyed every second as it washed over him. As the bathroom quickly filled with steam, he pictured himself in a fancy spa. He might even spend the morning lounging around in his fancy White Stuff waffle robe and slippers. Having his husband away from home really was relaxing.

James would often take the opportunity to have a quick wank during his daily shower, especially if he hadn't got lucky with Daniel the night before. But it was quite late this morning already, and the potential of Cleo waking up and interrupting was far too off-putting. Habits like this, however, are hard to stop, and even the thought of playing with it made his dick twitch. His penis had a mind of its own at the best of times, let alone when he was naked and lathered up.

No, not today. He really should get out before he heard the telltale screams of a little boy needing to be fed, changed, or entertained. At least if he had time before Cleo woke, he could enjoy a cuppa and his breakfast in peace.

Reluctantly turning off the water, he swept his hands from over his head, his neck and then all the way down to his groin. There it was, *almost* ready to go. Tempting, but it would have to wait until another time.

Shaking off as much excess water as he could, he opened the shower door to reach for a towel.

"Billy!" he screamed.

Billy stood frozen, halfway in, halfway out of the bathroom, with his hand on the door handle and a look of dread on his face. He was clearly as shocked as James was to be in such a predicament.

Mirroring him, James was on the lip of the shower tray, with his hand on the glass door. Fully naked, and still semi-erect. Although, after this little invasion, his semi was shrivelling fast.

A really awkward moment passed by silently before either of them could say anything.

Against his better judgement, Billy couldn't help but drop his gaze. He certainly hadn't done it intentionally, after all, James was his oldest and closest friend. Like a moth to the flame, on their own accord, his eyes dropped down to James' dick and his mouth drooped open.

"Shit! Shit shit shit. I'm SO sorry!" Billy shouted, covering his eyes with his free hand. Shocked and embarrassed, he then said, before he could stop himself, "lucky Daniel."

"Oh, shit," he repeated, so embarrassed he still couldn't move.

Fumbling to reach for his towel, James tripped over himself. Grasping onto the shower handle with all his weight, he pulled the door clean off his hinges as he fell to the floor.

"Ouch, fucking hell, that's heavy," he screamed as it

crashed into his leg.

"You want some help?" Billy asked, seriously concerned that James had done some real damage to himself. It was a glass door, after all.

James declined the offer, and quickly shooed him out of the bathroom, all before he could even reach for his towel.

Fucking hell! How could he have forgotten that Billy was staying over?

***

Even as early as it was, the day was already hot, sunny, and bright. With other priorities, Daniel would be unable to enjoy it properly. Instead, Daniel had been in his workshop since seven this morning. The effects of last night's alcohol had barely left any trace on him. He was so used to it nowadays, he rarely suffered from a hangover even after drinking far more than he had last night. But then, he probably lived in a constant state of having at least the remnants of a bottle or two circulating through his veins at any one time.

Right on cue, Duncan let himself in via the front door at eight thirty. As usual, he'd cycled down, wearing those tight-fitting exercise shorts of his that revealed everything. Daniel often wondered if his only employee wore them on purpose just to tease him.

"Morning Dan!" he'd shouted, upbeat.

"Morning Duncan," he replied with a smile, greeting him in on the shop floor.

He couldn't help but take another look at that bulge. Daniel was a gay man, after all, and it was a hell of a large bulge. It was only natural.

"You must be pleased," Daniel said, shaking the thought of it from his mind.

"Huh?" Duncan asked, rather confused.

"The football yesterday? James said he saw you. You won, didn't you?"

"Ah, yes. It was a decent match. We played well," he smiled proudly, as if he'd somehow been accountable for the win.

"Out with anyone I know?" Daniel asked curiously.

"Nope. No one you know..." Duncan replied casually before going off to change into his work clothes. Daniel stopped what he was doing and let his mind wander again.

Duncan was a handsome guy. Really good looking, in fact. Only twenty-one, but he took his job seriously, learning everything he could from Daniel. Tall, thin but muscular, he had dark skin and short, cropped afro hair. Daniel was surprised he wasn't seeing someone already. Although he was keen to know who he'd been drinking with, he didn't want to press the matter further.

***

After getting dressed and taking painkillers for the large bruise forming on his calf muscle, the first thing James did was call his husband. The shower door was now completely broken – fortunately not shattered, but fixing it was definitely a job left best for the handy one in the house. After all, James trying to re-hang it would make things *much* worse, he was sure. Billy had kindly offered to help, but in reality, he'd have probably done a poorer job than even James could.

James had tried several times to phone Daniel, but to no avail. Reluctantly opting to text his husband about the problem, minus the part about Billy seeing him starkers, his frustration rose when all he got back was a measly, 'You'll have to make do and I'll fix it when I get back.'

So much for asking if I'd hurt myself.

Taking his mind off his rather selfish, completely work-obsessed husband, James instead turned his attention to his house guest and the big news of the day.

Billy had mentioned something last night about having someone over today, but the details were a little hazy after their wine, so he couldn't quite remember the who, why and when of the visit.

"Now, are you sure you don't mind Dana coming over here?" Billy asked again, "because it's not too late for me to take her out for a coffee instead. We could even go for lunch or, for a walk, or something... don't feel like you have to stay, either, if you don't want to that is, I mean, you're obviously welcome to stay, it's your house and all..."

Billy could be as clumsy with his words as he was with his body. It was endearing, if not a little frustrating at times, although James had learned long ago to overlook it.

"If you don't mind, I'll stay. I can't wait to meet her,

actually. I still can't believe you haven't told Aiken about it yet, though."

Their earlier slightly awkward, rather amusing mishap long forgotten, Billy had helped by getting Cleo up and ready, and had kindly made breakfast for all three of them. James was surprised, but very grateful for the assistance. He couldn't remember the last time he'd had Cleo taken care of and his breakfast on the table like this. And if he'd have known, he'd have spent longer in the shower! That said, Billy walking in on him doing *that* would have been far worse than their already embarrassing encounter. There was naked, and then there was being caught pulling-one-off naked.

Taking a bite out of his huge croissant, James sat back and enjoyed his meal. Cleo was bouncing up and down on Uncle Billy's knee, and everyone was relaxed and happy. Who knew mornings could be so calm and peaceful?

I could really get used to this, thought James, looking over at the scene of blissful harmony.

"I wanted it to be a surprise. It's so stressful, and he's so busy. I really want to do all of the legwork on it first. I can vet her, well, *we* can vet her. You know, check she's okay and have everything worked out before I bother Aiken with it. You know what he's like."

"Yeah. About as busy as Daniel, I imagine. Are you sure you actually want to go through with this though? He probably won't be much help with it all," James warned from experience. Although in reality he knew exactly how much Billy wanted it, and what lengths he'd go to get it.

"I know, I'm not really expecting him to be. But you know how desperate I am for a child, and I think this is going to be easier than spending years waiting for the adoption agency to *possibly* pick us over a million aging straight couples."

"What time did you say she was coming over?"

"In an hour. But you know what lesbians are like. I wouldn't be surprised if she rocked up half an hour early and then complained that the coffee wasn't brewed. Oh my God, I'm so nervous. Maybe I should just cancel right now? I don't think I can take the pressure."

The crease in his brow said it all. James hated seeing his friend so worked up like this. Dana, the potential surrogate, probably wouldn't be thinking twice. Not worried, or concerned, or on edge at all. But for Billy, the one desperate for a child, this meant everything to him and he clearly wanted every little detail to be perfect.

"You'll be fine. I promise."

James knew how it felt. He was the same with the adoption agency. Always on tenterhooks, usually feeling like you weren't good enough. But then, in both scenarios, you're getting every minute detail of your lives judged from under a microscope. Does the state think you'll be good enough parents? Will a stranger become part of your family and carry your baby for you? The process was going to be so intense. James could tell how emotionally draining it had already been for Billy, and this is before his surrogate has even agreed to do it, let alone actually brought a child into the world for them.

***

It was a busy morning in Coben Oak. Daniel had been flat out in the workshop, progressing through an order of a full bedroom suite for one of his more affluent regulars. Duncan had been left out front to deal with a steady supply of customers, only coming through to catch up with Daniel intermittently.

"So how was your weekend?" he asked, coming through to offer up a cup of coffee.

He knew just how Daniel liked it.

"Hmm, great. Thanks," he said, taking the mug, and his first break in over three hours. "Yeah, it was good. Just a normal Saturday night, you know. But then, I did move out yesterday."

"You've left James?" Duncan asked, rather surprised this wasn't the very first thing he mentioned this morning. "Really?"

"Yup. Packed my bags and moved out last night. I'm staying at Aiken's for the week, and Billy has moved in to mine."

"Huh. I don't get it?"

"We've switched houses."

"Oh, you mean like a husband swap, then?" Duncan said, after the penny dropped.

"Yeah. They were joking on about it on Saturday night after a few bottles, but actually, with me being so busy this week anyway, it seemed like a good idea. It'll mean I can stay here as long as I need to without James nagging me."

"Ahh. Yeah, I guess that makes sense," he agreed with a smile, knowing how often Daniel would be chased by his husband to get home early on an evening. "Do you still want me to stay after closing?"

"Sure, yeah. If you can. We have so much to get through in a short space of time. That would really help me out, if you don't mind."

Not only was Duncan happy for the overtime, but he appreciated the time and dedication Daniel was putting into teaching him the trade. Living alone, he didn't have a partner or even a pet to take care of and although he had a packed social life, he enjoyed being in the workshop as much as anywhere else. It was definitely time well spent, in his opinion.

Duncan didn't mind spending all that extra time with his boss, either.

***

"Come in, come in. I'm so glad to finally meet you," Billy said eagerly, with his heart in his mouth.

He'd been pacing up and down the living room for the last half an hour, nervously flitting between excitement and nausea. He literally couldn't sit down. This was such a big deal for him, and he'd rehearsed every conceivable conversation with her in his head. But now, he felt his mind was at a blank and he didn't really have a clue what to say.

Dana wasn't what Billy expected. Not by a long shot.

Since leaving their clubbing days behind, the boys' circles were no longer on the scene, and neither Billy nor James had any lesbian friends to compare her to. They often joked about lesbians wearing checked shirts with short hair, and being keen golfers, but Dana wasn't like this at all. She was so *pedestrian*, so 'normal looking' it was refreshing, he figured. Billy scorned himself for being so naïve, and apparently homophobic towards the fairer sex, too.

Lesbians are people too, Billy. He could almost hear Aiken scorning him from beyond.

Long, mousey brown hair, barely any makeup. Jeans and a little blouse. She was forgettably pretty, but in a nice way. She seemed a perfectly respectable young woman, if not a tiny bit rough around the edges. Certainly not the worse choice when thinking about the looks of his future offspring, should she also offer to donate her eggs too.

Billy's heart was racing. He was so excited he felt like he could wet himself.

"You must be Aiken. What a lovely couple you make," she said as Billy led her through to the lounge.

"Ah Dana, nice to meet you. Nope, I'm the best friend, not the husband. He's shacked up with *my* husband this week."

"James! What the..." Billy blushed, mortified, as he whacked him on the shoulder. "What he means is, both of our husbands are busy working this week, so I've come here to keep him company and help him with baby Cleo."

Maybe she'll appreciate the fact I'm getting in extra practice, he hoped.

"Ahh. No problem," she said, with her face relaxing a touch.

"Really," Billy muttered to James under his breath. He was nervous enough, without the fear of Dana being put off the very first minute she'd arrived.

"Can I get you a drink?" James offered, excusing himself as quickly as possible.

He knew how much this meant to Billy, and he wouldn't be able to forgive himself if he'd already buggered it up for him.

***

In one of his own shops, much like Daniel, Aiken was rushed off his feet. *Flowers by Stead* was the premiere name in floristry for at least a hundred and fifty-miles in any direction, and Aiken hadn't earned that title by sitting idle. Over the last ten years, he'd built up an empire (as Billy always called it) of six shops, and had personally trained each of his managers.

Obviously, he was very particular about the talents and abilities of his staff, just as much as he was about the flowers they sold and the bouquets they made. He was a good businessman, a great florist, and took pride in everything he did.

However, experiencing certain problems with the lease of his flagship store, he'd had to temporarily move out, unfortunately. The shop had on more than one occasion been labelled as the 'jewel of the town's high street'. And he was desperate to get back in, where he belonged. Whilst problems with the landlord were being ironed out, he'd decided to make his base in one of his smaller, more rural shops out of town. At least this one had a larger stockroom and, therefore, a little bit more space for him to work his magic.

"Thanks, Silvie," he said, receiving his coffee.

Even though it was still his shop, albeit one of his satellite branches, he felt a little out of his comfort zone. He almost felt like he was stepping on her toes, but he supposed it was good for staff morale and team building to spend time with colleagues he wasn't used to working with on a daily basis. He'd personally interviewed every single employee, but that didn't mean they were overly familiar with working side by side with him.

"You're welcome. Wow, stunning," she beamed.

Slightly taken aback, he thought it a little odd of her to be flirting with him. She *definitely* knew he was gay. *Didn't she?*

With a slight pang of abandonment, he couldn't help but be reminded of how Billy would regularly complement him – to the point of rather losing its poignancy. Then he realised what she meant.

"Oh, the flowers, of course. Thank you! I was intending to use a display like this for the new website, and maybe a few oversized pictures behind the desk."

He finished by gently placing the last large blue poppy just off centre, before taking a step back to admire his work.

A smatter of blue in a spray of white and green. Simple.

Timeless. Perfect.

No sooner had Silvie left him to return to the front desk, Aiken had heard the front door chime ring out. From the muffled conversations in the next room, he picked out a voice that he recognised very well.

Oh Dear.

He left his arrangement and went to face the music.

"Broderick, my old friend. How are you doing?" He beamed hollowly.

"Very well thank you," he replied, leaning in to read her name badge. "Silvie here was just taking care of me."

"Why don't you come through the back for a cup of tea?" Aiken reluctantly suggested.

He could guess what Broderick was after and there was no way he wanted to have any of that conversation in front of anyone, let alone his employee, Silvie.

With an arm around one of his oldest friends, he led Broderick through to the back and closed the door.

***

Billy was enjoying getting to know Dana. Once the initial nervousness dissipated, he quickly fell into a comfortable flow of conversation, with Dana going out of her way to make it so easy for him. He was grateful of James being there too, asking questions that he may have forgotten to cover, and likewise mentioning things about the couple that he may be too modest to own up to. He had to make a great first impression and Billy thought that James, putting his foot in it initially aside, was doing just that.

Dana had put them both at ease really early on. She told them, still talking as though they were having a child together, that she understood. She'd worked with several couples before, both gay and straight, and she knew how difficult and scary the process was. She promised she'd be as helpful as possible and would be with them every step of the way. They could contact her any time, day or night if anything was bothering them, on their mind, or if they just wanted to talk about it, because she knew how important it was that they were a part of everything. She beamed as she spoke. A people person, she was the perfect woman to do this for Billy and Aiken, he just knew it.

Dana had to remind herself more than once that they weren't a couple, and that this wasn't their family home. James had stressed that Billy's house was even nicer than his, which she thought was impressive enough, and although neither one of them said it explicitly, it was clear that Billy and his husband had some money behind them. After all, by what they had told her, Billy's husband was a really successful businessman.

Dana didn't, *couldn't*, charge for what she was offering to do for them, but that didn't mean it wasn't an expensive process, regardless. Doctor's visits, antenatal classes, vitamins and other health supplements, the list just went on.

After two cups of tea, a slice of cake and what felt like a hundred garibaldis, Dana left James' house with smiles all around.

She liked James. It was a shame that he wasn't with Billy. She thought they really would have been a perfect couple. After only an hour and a half it felt like she'd got to know both of them pretty well, and felt certain that Billy, with or without James' help, would make the perfect parent.

She just couldn't wait to get back home and tell her husband all about it.

***

There wasn't much space in the stockroom, but Aiken was pacing back and forth nonetheless.

After listening to Broderick's spiel, he paused and finally said, "You've got it wrong."

Broderick made an effort to sigh. "I'm telling you; *you've* got it wrong. I'm actually trying to help you here."

"But I don't want your help. I don't need it. We're doing just fine," he lied.

Many years ago, Broderick and Aiken had been the best of friends. They'd trained together, learning the art of their craft, long before either one of them had opened their first boutique. They had big plans, both of them, and had often talked about going into it together. It could have been amazing.

Instead, due to a series of snap decisions that neither one of them could remember who'd made, they had gone their separate ways. Slowly growing apart as friends, they somehow became low-key rivals as their budding businesses fought for customers. As time progressed, *Flowers by Stead* had eventually taken the lead. Clearly Broderick wasn't one to give up without a fight.

"Cut the crap Aiken. I've heard the rumours. I've seen your High Street shop close down. It's only a matter of time now anyway, before that'll be up for rental."

"That's a problem with the landlord, not me."

"Whatever you say. Anyway, I don't want to fight anymore. I never came here to fight. We were friends once. Let me help you out. I can make this much easier for you."

"Will you please keep your voice down? I don't want you scaring Silvie."

Broderick shook his head in frustration. He then took out one of his impeccably smart business cards from his breast pocket. Taking a pen from the tiny desk in the corner of the room, he wrote something on it and placed it face down on the workbench under Aiken's bouquet.

"This is my offer for all six shops and your trading name. I'm sure that will sort you out." He took Aiken by the shoulders and held his stare. It almost seemed that his concern was genuine. "Just think about it."

Broderick took one last glance at Aiken. With a sad smile, he patted him on the back and let himself out.

Aiken closed the door behind him. He took a deep breath and lifted the card to find out his worth.

The Previous Tuesday

Six

In the early hours of the morning, the bedroom door slowly crept open with a squeak, rousing James from his dream. A sliver of moonlight just illuminating the thin vertical patch of wall next to the doorframe. Tired and still half asleep, at first he assumed it was Cleo, who must have somehow climbed out of his cot. Strange he wasn't calling out though. Then James registered the shadow, blocking out most of the light from the hall. Tall and large. *Daniel?*

But he's not here...

Billy?

Gently, the door closed behind the shadow and the room was plunged back into complete and total darkness.

Moments later, the covers were pulled back and James could feel the weight of someone climbing in on Daniel's side of the bed.

Sure, they'd had another couple of bottles of wine between them last night, but Billy wasn't drunk enough to make a stupid mistake, like trying to climb in next to James. *Was he?*

Nothing yet had been said, but James could feel his pulse quicken and his flaccid phallus twitch, just a little. He scorned himself for going there; about thinking of such things in relation to his oldest pal. He rolled over, burrowing his head into his pillow. This was his best friend. Nothing was going to happen. They didn't have to worry about shit like this.

Maybe Billy was just lonely? Or cold? Maybe he'd been sleepwalking and didn't even know what he was doing. Anything was possible when you were so tired.

Then an arm wrapped itself around James and pulled him closer from behind. There was no doubt about who was in his bed now. The sweet breezy scent of *Abercrombie & Fitch;* Billy's signature and only aftershave.

Billy mumbled something indecipherable and slowly ground his erection into the small of James' back.

Fuck. Not only had he got into bed with James, but he wasn't wearing pants, either... and by all accounts, it was big.

This had already gone too far. Regardless of absent husbands and overstrung libidos, this would be crossing a line both of them would well and truly regret in the morning, no matter how fun it might be in the moment.

Giving into temptation just a little longer, James ground back into the warmth of Billy. Slowly circling his hips, he began to massage Billy's cock with his buttocks, desperate to feel the tip of his hardness at one of his most erogenous zones. His own cock was now firmly erect and ready to join the party.

This was too much. He couldn't. Even with the excuse of alcohol, he couldn't go further. *Could he?*

James rolled over to face Billy, to decline his advances and to put an end to it before anything serious happened. But he'd been wrong. It wasn't Billy in there next to him. Somehow, Kirk had snuck into bed with him.

Kirk.

The ex.

Kirk the bastard. Kirk the amazing fuck, that had always held some kind of sexual allure over James.

He kissed James deeply. With a rough forcefulness that James had missed, he pulled him close with a broad hand on his behind. The feel of his touch sent throbbing sensations throughout James' entire body.

This was so wrong, but it felt so amazing to be wanted like this, to be desired sexually...

Kirk rolled himself on top. Like he used to all those years ago, he pinned James' arms above his head, firmly into the mattress. He liked to take charge. He liked to be dominant. To have his way with James, who revelled at the weight of his ex, sat naked on his chest. That cock of his which was inching ever closer to James' face. Within seconds, Kirk had forcefully shoved it down his throat with a deep thrusting motion. The warmth radiating from Kirk's groin was incredible. James couldn't help but run a hand up, cupping Kirk's hairy balls, before sliding his fingers up and wrapping them around the base of his thick shaft.

James ebbed closer to climax at the sheer thought of having sex with the one and only man he couldn't stand to be around under any other circumstance.

There was an undeniable chemistry; fiery, animalistic, and raw. The sex was always amazing, but after so many years apart, this now felt exquisite. Without ever expecting it, this was clearly the fantasy that James had been craving for so long.

A cry from outside of his bedroom instantly broke the illusion.

He groggily shook his head, trying to get his bearings... forcing himself to wake up fully.

A dream.

Of course it was a dream.

Fucking hell, that was one of the hottest dreams I've had in years, though.

Reaching for the bedside lamp, he then turned to check... just to make sure. Yes, his bed was empty, but he *had* to make sure after such an intensely passionate fantasy like that.

Sitting up momentarily, he listened out for Cleo. Would he need to get up, or was it just a bad dream already forgotten? A few more minutes of silence and he turned off the light and shuffled back down under the covers, hopeful that there'd be no more noise from his son tonight. Hopefully, he might even be able to enjoy himself, now he knew he wasn't actually cheating on his husband.

Wow, he must be suffering from withdrawal symptoms if he was having wet dreams about Billy *and* Kirk, James thought as he tried to drift back off.

He had to admit, it was hot, though. He also had to admit the idea of having a secret midnight rendezvous with his best friend and his last 'mistake' was tantalising. It brought back those painfully angst years of puberty where James noticed Billy for the first time, but didn't quite know why. At the time, Billy was so far back in the closet he had no idea himself about sexuality or what it meant to be gay. Lots had changed in the twenty-plus years, and it felt so wrong to think of his best friend in this context.

The trouble Kirk had caused him and Daniel, that wasn't worth revisiting for anything in real life, but under the safety of his own dreams and fantasies, the thought was too hot to resist.

Still half asleep, but now fully hard himself, James gave into temptation and fantasised about Billy fucking him from behind, with Kirk roughly taking the lead in front.

He imagined Billy's fuller, hairy body. Big, strong and masculine. He could feel Billy's chest hair tickle his back as they spooned. Further down, a really big dick was poking him, edging its way in, wet with pre-cum.

Kirk was facing him, rubbing his hard cock up and down his leg as he pushed his lips onto James. The imagined weight and pressure from their naked bodies front and back was so fucking hot. A hot sweaty tangle of arms, legs, torsos, and cocks rubbing up against one another, all destined to end up sticky with semen.

He pictured Billy kissing behind his ear, nuzzling into his neck, whilst Kirk reached down to take James' cock in his hand. Fucking for the sake of it, enjoying it and being pleasured, not just coming as quickly as possible to get it over and done with, as was usual whenever Daniel had given the green light.

James imagined Kirk's strong hands all over him, squeezing, pulling, and caressing his naked body. There was pain mixed in there, too. A rough hand squeezing his ass, a tug on his nipple and then firm, dominating fingers around his throat...

What James would give in this moment – just for this moment, for it all to be actually happening. It was wicked and wrong, but that just made him want it even more. He'd spent years dreaming of having sex like this when he was a teenager, and had wasted years later on actually fucking like this with Kirk... and to have Billy literally sleeping in the room next door, with both of them husbandless and alone... it was almost too much. If Billy had walked in right now, James knew there would be nothing he could do to stop the inevitable from happening. To see his cock in real life... to taste it, just once... if only Kirk was here too.

James imagined Kirk forcefully rolling him back and onto Billy's stomach. Now on top of both of them. Kirk thrust himself into James, who was already tightly filled by Billy. The pain would be immense, but the act itself exquisite.

As soon as James came, the shame and regret of what he'd just fantasised about played heavily on his mind.

How could I sexualise my best friend like that, just for a quick wank?

This is Billy, for God's sake. It's sooo wrong to think of him like that, but wow...

And more to the point, how could I sexualise Kirk like that at all, after what he'd done to me?

***

By the following morning, James had calmed down a little and had pushed last night's imaginary dalliance to one side. It was far better to pretend it hadn't happened. Most guys occasional fantasised about people they shouldn't, *didn't they?* It's not like he actually *did* anything, he reasoned. After all, it was just his heightened sexuality wanting something to think about. If he'd have been having regular sex with his own husband, there would have been no need to think about his friends, or enemies, in such ways.

Although today quite randomly, he couldn't help but notice that Billy was looking particularly adorable, with his messy bed-hair and his big doe eyes... even for first thing in the morning. Sat in his dressing gown, across the breakfast table, he'd made absolutely no effort (obviously there wasn't a need to) but he just looked good, so relaxed and comfortable like that, with his big teddy bear grin. Billy really did suit being the non-scene, non-pretentious 'normal' gay guy that he was. Just a cute, nice-looking man with a big smile and a heart of gold. It worked in his favour that he didn't have that arrogant confidence of Daniel. It just wasn't his style at all, fortunately.

However wrong it was to think of Billy being attractive, it definitely beat thinking about Kirk at all.

"I thought you were working today?" James asked, clearing his gullet with a little cough.

For some reason there was a slight touch of nervousness in his voice. Not quite butterflies, or the feeling of guilt about last night... maybe he just had a frog in his throat.

"I am. Working a full day today. I start at nine. Still got plenty of time. Ba bababa baa..." Billy said absentmindedly as he pulled faces at Cleo.

"Are you sure about that?"

...

"Billy..."

"Yeah?"

"I said, are you sure you have plenty of time? It's eight twenty. You're still in a robe and you work at least half an hour away."

"Shit shit shit!" he said, jumping up, dropping his phone as he fussed.

He knocked his toe on the leg, and then banged his head on the underside of the table as he picked it up.

"Bee Yee," Cleo shouted, upset his entertainment was leaving.

"Sorry. I mean 'Oops' Cleo. James, would you mind giving me a lift? I'll never get a parking space now," he shouted, running upstairs to get dressed.

Well, he's certainly made himself at home.

James figured that without a child, and with Aiken working all the time, there wasn't much for Billy to miss back home. His house was amazing, but that never beat having it filled with family. He'd clearly settled into his new routine with such ease. It was nice to see.

Billy almost kissed the top of James' head as he left the kitchen, before muttering something awkwardly about it being a force of habit with Aiken.

James blushed, letting the comment go unanswered.

***

Across town, Daniel had made himself as comfortable as Billy had.

"Sorry for keeping you up so late last night," he said to his host apologetically.

"You didn't, no bother at all. I was actually going to head off to work in a minute, but if you fancy a coffee, I can stick around a little longer," Aiken offered.

To be honest, Aiken was keen for the company. Although he never carried an air of superiority at work by any means, it often felt a little strange talking to his assistants, or even his shop managers with certain aspects of his life. He liked to keep things close to his chest even around friends, so was particularly keen to separate his work life from his personal life when he was in the shop. Although he wouldn't admit it, it was probably a shyness about being openly gay, yet not liking being judged for it.

Although Aiken and Daniel weren't the best friends that James and Billy were, due to their current circumstances, they were at least, literally, quite close. It would be good for them to get to know each other better and build on what they'd learnt about one another over the years. With very different personalities, it was a stretch, but who knew, they may become proper friends by the end of the week.

"Sure. I *was* aiming to be in for seven today, but with such a late night, I think I earned at least a bit of a lie in. I did manage to get a lot done yesterday evening, though, so I deserve it. Honestly, I can't tell you how nice it is not to be woken up by a kid screaming in the middle of the night."

"I don't fancy that at all."

"Well, you've got it all to come, my friend," Daniel grinned, reaching across the table with his empty cup.

Aiken filled it, filled another mug for himself, and sat back down opposite his guest. He wasn't responsible for opening up the shop, and as it was his business, he had no one to answer to. So what if he came in a little later than Silvie was expecting?

"We'll see. It might not even happen. To be honest, I'm happy with things exactly the way they are. I'm not sure bringing a baby into the mix is such a great idea," he said, crumpling his brow. "After all, finances could change at any minute, especially running my own business. It's not like we could live off Billy's salary, even without a child," he justified.

"True. I mean, we're the same... and James doesn't work at all. I totally get it. But Billy, he doesn't shut up about the adoption or surrogacy or whatever it is you two are going to do to have a baby. He's desperate for it, isn't he?"

"I know, I know... but the agency told us we'd probably be waiting years, if it happens at all. I told him if we haven't been matched by the time I'm forty-five, then it's too late. I've been honest and up front about it since day one. I don't want to be one of those geriatric parents who are forced to work up until the day they die just to send their kids to university."

"I don't blame you. I'd never go for another now. One's more than enough for me, even if James wants more. I love the little fella, but I wouldn't put myself through that again, I can tell you. It's got to be a balance, right? And sometimes, kids throw that balance right out of the window. And James, he doesn't have the time to even go to the gym at the moment. I guess it must frustrate him too."

Daniel was a hard one to crack, too, thought Aiken. He was sure that he loved his son. Who wouldn't with a kid like Cleo? He said all of the right words, continued to sing his praises, but Aiken wasn't sure if this was as much lip service as anything else. He never saw Daniel lift a finger. He hadn't heard any stories about Daniel getting covered in food whilst feeding him, or poo whilst changing his nappy. It's like he was a 1950s dad who was there to make money, tell his wife she was pretty and not a lot else. How close could you really get to a child without putting in the effort?

That was another concern of Aiken's to add to the list: Would he even have the time to be a good father? Although he wasn't sure about kids in the first place, he was determined to do the best job he could if the day ever arrived. That would definitely have a negative impact on him running his business, wouldn't it?

The pair finished their coffees, happy to joke about enjoying the serenity that was left in the wake of their absent husbands.

***

"Come on then, how's it going so far?" she asked with an expectant grin.

"I don't know what you mean," James said as if butter wouldn't melt.

Killing his boredom whilst Billy was at work today, he had taken Cleo around to his mum's house. None of the other stay at home parents were free and he knew his mum always appreciated a visit.

Nana Kath was besotted with her only grandson. As a recently retired teacher that didn't want to be reported to the authorities by hanging around playgrounds to get her fix of small children, Cleo was definitely her preferred option. She really missed her kids at school, but was now pleased to spend as much time as possible with him instead.

"You mark my words, there'll be fireworks," she warned, raising her eyebrow knowingly.

"Nannnann, nannannna... Caarrr!" Cleo shouted enthusiastically, running over to her.

"Yes darling, it's a car."

"What could you possibly mean by that, Mum?"

"Come off it... you know very well what I'm getting at," she said, picking Cleo up to bounce him on her lap. "This is the way the lady rides..."

Ever the wriggler, she managed to get one big kiss in from him before he was off again looking for other toys in the conservatory. There had been a neatly packed box of goodies in the corner when the pair arrived, but most of its contents were now scattered across the room as though a tornado had swept through the house. In fact, that was a rather appropriate description of Cleo when he was awake.

"It's fine. Obviously, it's fine. Why wouldn't it be?"

"Well, I'm just saying. Watch yourself–"

"With what?" he interjected, trying to act as though he didn't understand where she was coming from.

"You know what I'm talking about, love. For about eighteen months straight, you used to follow Billy around. Anything he did, you wanted to do. Anything he wore, you wanted. He cut his hair, you had to do the same. You were besotted with him."

"I did not!" James protested firmly.

His mum just raised a single eyebrow. It said everything. There was little point in arguing back as they both knew it was true.

"Oh, c'mon. I was fifteen, *Mother*; I didn't know what I wanted back then."

"And then what happened?" she asked, ignoring him. "You eventually got bored of him and the minute you were interested in someone else, he started to like you."

"What? I don't think so. He's never been interested in me... and I only liked him like that because I had a stupid childish crush, which I obviously grew out of decades ago. We are best friends. Nothing more."

"I saw the way he looked at you. As soon as you started dating Mark, you could tell he'd realised what he was missing. He'd finally realised he liked you, and then what? You were already dating someone else, and there was a long string of guys after Mark..."

Kath pursed her lips slightly as she ever so gently rolled her eyes. It was the typical 'I told you so' manoeuvre that was so subtle James had no way of pulling her up for it. That didn't mean he hadn't noticed it though.

"You make me sound terrible! Anyway, Billy has never been interested in me like that. We're best friends. We have been since we've been kids. And if you haven't forgotten, we are both happily married now and I have a child."

"I know that, love, but I also see that Daniel doesn't always give you enough of the attention you need. Plus, I know how much you boys like to drink. I just don't want you to make a silly mistake when you're feeling tipsy, only to regret it all later."

"Oh my God, this conversation is awful, Mother. Can we please stop dissecting my love life? I'm happily married to Daniel. Billy is happily married to Aiken and we're all very happy being friends. This was just a fun week whilst Daniel has to work."

"If you say so."

"I do."

"Just be careful," she added, not quite able to help herself.

"Mother!" he said with the usual tone required for his mum at her nosiest. Desperate to change the subject by any means necessary, he brought up the dreaded ex. "Anyway, you'll never guess who's back?"

"Kirk?"

The look of surprise on his face was a picture. Mouth wide open, eyebrows raised. He never saw that one coming.

"How in the hell did you know that he was back?"

"I saw him on Saturday. I wasn't going to mention it, but since you brought it up..."

"Why wouldn't you have told me? You could have at least given me a warning. I was totally unprepared. He caught me off guard and loved every minute of it."

"It's bad enough that you've got your childhood crush living with you whilst your husband is away working. Please promise me you won't get involved with Kirk again. He was nothing but trouble and that would all end in tears, believe me."

As if.

As if James would ever be that stupid to wreck his whole life with that arsehole, however good the sex might have been. He'd nearly lost Daniel once to Kirk, and he was adamant it would not happen again.

Kath got herself up from the couch to go and put the kettle on. She really did worry about her son sometimes. He had always been an affectionate little boy. Sensitive and caring. Although she could see straight away why he'd fallen for Daniel – who, she reminded herself, had been a great provider for the family - she wondered if James could truly be happy with someone like that. Someone who couldn't, or didn't want to, give him the affection he craved. Even after more than a decade of them being together, she still wondered if her son was truly happy.

Now she worried that he needed the one thing Daniel wasn't good at, and with him being away for a whole week, was the pull of his closest confidant (and previous crush), or the bad boy that had broken his heart more than once, too much to resist?

James had been known to make catastrophic errors with his love life before, after all.

"Cleo, do you want to help Nana make a cake?" she called out, trying to put those concerns to the back of her mind.

***

Daniel and Duncan had both had another busy day at work. It was a productive, but exhausting shift and they were both tired. Unfortunately, there was still a lot more to do before the end of the week. Exactly as Daniel had expected. He shouldn't complain. His business being so busy was a good thing, he knew, it was just exhausting at times, especially when he wasn't getting enough sleep.

Although he loved his family, he didn't miss James' constant nagging. *Where are you? When will you be home? Cleo is missing you...* the guilt trips never ended, so it was far easier to just not go back at all sometimes. He really was grateful that Aiken was putting him up for the week. Why hadn't he thought of a setup like this much sooner? Maybe they could even make it a regular thing, every now and again?

Duncan had just shut up for the day and had made his way through to the back. "Anything I can help with?"

"Are you kidding? There's still a lot to do... that is, if you don't mind sticking around again?"

"Of course not."

"I was thinking..." Daniel began, "it'll be another late night again, for me at least. So rather than me traipsing back and waking Aiken up, only to come back here first thing, it probably it makes more sense for me just stay across the road, at the Cedar Court Inn."

Duncan raised an eyebrow. "I guess. Would you like me to book it for you?" he offered with a smile.

"Please. You know, depending how long you're able to hang around for, maybe I could take you out, my treat... we could grab a bite to eat and a quick drink there at around eight before coming back here?"

"Sounds like a plan."

As he was staying late to help out in the workshop again, Duncan wasted no time in stripping down to his waist before looking for something more suitable to wear. He wasn't shy half naked and was quite happy to strut around showing off what he had. He even liked the attention from Daniel, who tried his best not to show his interest, but failed miserably.

It was just too hard. When Duncan looked as he did, Daniel had little control over where his eyes wandered.

Duncan knew. He also knew that most of the gay guys he'd met also liked to look at him. He'd been used to the attention since puberty, and in honesty he liked it. All the more when it came from his *Dilf* boss.

Due to the mess that was usually made in the workshop, they kept an array of spare clothes hung up, just in case. A last-minute business meeting with a new client, a touch up of varnish on something just to be sold or an afternoon on the shopfloor. They didn't always know what the day ahead would entail.

Reaching for his overalls, Duncan didn't want to ruin his 'good' clothes with wood glue, oil, stain or anything else he might find himself covered in this evening...

Seven

It had been a long and laborious day in *Steamy Beanz* coffee shop. They always dragged out painfully when business was so quiet. In the heat of the summer, people were less inclined to be in town asking for hot beverages and far more inclined to head to the beach with a cool refreshing beer. Who could blame them?

Billy's shift would have dragged like crazy if it hadn't been for Sandie this afternoon. The pair had managed a proper catch up, and a good laugh, even if it had been uncomfortably hot for them.

Sandie knew just how to make Billy laugh when they worked together and they had no problem in finding even the most mundane things to entertain themselves between customers. Neither of them would be considered particularly professional at the best of times, but when they were together, any sense of maturity or propriety was thrown out of the window. It was a surprise they were still allowed to work together, in all honesty. Their game this afternoon had been spotting and judging the more colourful couples that had walked past the café window.

"Miss-match!", "Money Grabbing whore!", "Definitely cheating on him with his best friend!" Sandie was savage, but Billy couldn't deny that she was thoroughly entertaining.

By the time they had ushered the last of their customers out, cleaned around, counted up and closed up for the night, Billy was absolutely shattered.

He enjoyed the work, but he often found the long stints hard on his feet. Standing up all day, making small talk with ratty customers or the one or two colleagues he didn't like, it wasn't quite the easy ride that Aiken had taken it to be. If only jobs paid for the effort, rather than the education and training required, thought Billy. He'd be a millionaire several times over.

After promising Sandie they would have that long-overdue night out soon before saying goodbye to her, he texted James, offering to collect dinner. By seven-fifteen, he was letting himself in with a bottle of wine and a take-away for them to share.

"Hmmm, Thai. My favourite. I've got everything set," James greeted him at the door like a loyal dog to his master.

"Thank God, I'm knackered. I just wanna kick back with a glass of wine and a shitty film."

"You're in luck then," James grinned. The Anne Hathaway flick he'd chosen was just what the doctor ordered. With no concentration required, it suited both of them perfectly.

Still playing heavy on his mind, James had given in and decided to talk to Billy about Kirk, minus the sex dream that he was also starring in, of course. There was something called 'too much information' even between best friends, after all.

"Are you serious? He actually sauntered up to you, expecting you to welcome him back with open arms?" Billy asked, dumbfounded.

"I know. And, you know what... I just know he's after something. I could tell by the way he was acting. He had that lizard look in his eye that you always hated."

"Haha! Well, of course he's after *something*. When hasn't he been? Conniving little bastard, just out for what he can get. Do you think he wants to get back with you?"

"I'm not sure, but I definitely got that vibe from him. The way he was asking for an invite... fishing around for info, asking after me and Daniel... he even asked after you. Maybe he was more interested in you?" James suggested half-heartedly.

"Ha. Don't even start with that. First of all, you know he doesn't go for real men like me. Second off, there is no way I'd date someone with a forked tongue and a sub-human heart temperature. It'll be you he's wanting. But after what happened last time, it's not really a surprise, is it?"

"Just what I need right now; him hanging around whilst Daniel is away from home. God, why can't things ever go smoothly?"

"Tell me about it!" Billy groaned in agreement.

"Oh, that reminds me..." he mumbled to himself.

Dragging his phone out of his pocket, he texted his husband again. Complaining about the shower, pleading with him to pop by tomorrow to fix it. He was getting water everywhere every time he showered.

They'd drank sensibly whist watching the film, which meant only one bottle of wine *between them*, before calling it an evening. Walking upstairs and saying 'night' to each other, they joked about giving one another a goodnight kiss. It was all very domesticated and rather silly, but certainly nothing for James' mum to worry about for God's sake.

Billy couldn't wait to hit the pillow. There was so much to think about with regards to Dana and the baby. He'd been mulling over every single thing they had chatted about in his head since yesterday's meeting. *Had he said the right thing? Had James? Did she like him? Was she really going to get pregnant with his baby?*

Either way, she seemed really onboard, like she was totally keen to support them. That was the main thing at that stage, wasn't it? Just finding a surrogate that you got on with, that you could actually imagine doing this with.

But the next big question was, all things going well, how he was actually going to break the news to Aiken? And then, *when were they going to fall pregnant? What were they going to call the baby? Would they ever try for a second, and if they did, would Aiken insist on using the same surrogate?* Dana had already suggested she'd be keen to help them a second time, should they be interested, so it certainly wasn't off the cards.

It was exciting for sure, but without Aiken to talk to about it, he felt a little lonely.

He could talk to James about it all, at least. He always talked to James. In fact, even if he was living with Aiken and they hadn't swapped homes, he would probably have spoken to James about Dana first before his husband.

Billy thought again about James yesterday morning. How embarrassing, walking in on his best friend getting out of the shower like that. It wouldn't have been an issue if they were straight. Didn't straight guys do that all the time in locker rooms? It probably wouldn't have been such an issue even though they were gay if James hadn't had a stiffy, either, he guessed. It was that bit that made it awkward. The fact James was standing to attention. Well, swinging to attention, more accurately...

Bloody hell, Billy hadn't expected to see that first thing on a morning, but he had to admit it was rather impressive. Being the true gay man he was, Billy always appreciated a good cock shot, so one in the flesh was even better. He wasn't particularly fussy, or a size queen by any means, but he had to give it to James. He was packing some meat down there. *Lucky Daniel...*

It took no time at all for his own prick to catch up, ready to be played with at the sheer thought of James dripping off, half-erect in the shower. That and the fact he hadn't had sex in forever. This was Aiken's fault! If he wasn't so starved of the action, he'd barely have given it a second thought. Before he knew what he was doing, he'd wrapped his fingers around his shaft and, although already half asleep, had started massaging himself.

Husbands aside, a no-strings quicky with James would have been exciting. Of course, he would never actually do that; for many reasons, not least the fear of ruining a lifelong friendship. Nevertheless, it would have been fun just once. Particularly as Billy had never really played the field like a lot of other gay guys he knew.

Like himself, James was versatile. He also knew, like himself, that James didn't have the sex-life he sorely wanted. A no strings, *one-night* affair could have been perfect for both of them under different circumstances. Wow, that would be so hot.

Stroking his cock, he thought about James in the shower. That large dick of his, not quite hard, but still big and firm enough to make an impact. He thought about bending down and taking James in his mouth. Sliding back the skin and enjoying the fullness right down to the base of his balls.

It had been a long time since Billy had thought about anyone other than his husband or the porn stars he was watching online, and it felt kind of naughty. But it made him feel so guilty too, which only served to make the situation seem all the more desirable.

The things James and he would get up to, given half the chance...

With the tip of his cock already wet, Billy reached for a sock. He still felt wrong for masturbating in James' spare room, but he just couldn't hold out any longer. It was daft for any of them to expect him to, really. This was night three, after all. There was no chance he'd last until he back home.

Nobody in their right mind would have expected that from him.

The thought of his best friend walking in, catching him in the act, *joining him*, was too much to resist any longer.

Billy released what felt like a month's worth of pent-up semen over his abdomen. Hot and sticky, but satisfying. He mopped the mess up with his sock, rolled over, and fell into a well-earned and peaceful sleep.

***

Daniel clinked glasses with Duncan. "Thanks. I really wouldn't be able to manage this week without you."

"No problem. Happy to help!" He smiled genuinely.

They had just finished dinner and had taken a bottle of wine up to Daniel's hotel room. It certainly wasn't the smartest hotel in town. But it was clean, modern, and comfortable enough for Daniel to get a good night's sleep. With just one bedside light on, there was a very chilled ambiance in the room and the wine only helped to relax them further.

The intention was to head back across the road as soon as they were done and work a couple more hours. The sooner they got the orders complete and out, the better. Daniel would rather work hard and get the job done early, instead of letting it spill into the weekend or beyond. It was important to stay professional at all times and that usually meant under-promising and over-delivering. Much better that than those tradesmen who promised the world and rarely delivered on time, or to the high standards that they'd promised.

Daniel looked good. Sat on the edge of the bed, his sleeves were rolled up and his top two buttons were undone. Sneaking a glimpse, Duncan could just make out the outline of his pectoral muscles. Like him, Daniel worked hard to maintain an enviable physique, not only in the workshop but out running and in the gym too, by all accounts. And even though he was a little older, it still showed.

"You know what today is?" Duncan asked, very blasé as he swirled the wine around in his glass.

"Yes, I know what today is," Daniel grinned. "Why do you think I wanted to book the hotel room?"

Duncan took his cue and placed his glass down on the desk. Unhurried, he sauntered over to the edge of the bed. Pushing his boss down onto the mattress, he grinned. Slowly, Duncan unbuttoned the rest of Daniel's shirt until his chest was completely exposed. He then carefully straddled him before leaning over for a kiss.

"Our..." he kissed his lips.

"Two..." a kiss on Daniel's neck.

"Month..." another kiss, this time on his nipple.

"Anniversary," he finished, kissing him once more on his lips again.

Daniel took firm hold of Duncan, an arm in each hand, and boldly rolled him over onto his back. He knew Duncan liked it when he was rough. Sometimes even he liked playing up to the big boss routine.

"Our two-month anniversary, is it?" he asked playfully.

Duncan grinned and began to writhe, desperate to remove his own clothes.

"Well, I think that deserves a two-month anniversary fuck... don't you?"

Climbing up, Daniel stood up off the bed. He removed Duncan's trousers and underwear in one swift movement and flipped him over onto his front.

Daniel gave his tight brown arse a playful slap.

"Ouch!" Duncan called out, liking the attention. He was already relaxed and eager to take his lover's cock.

Daniel enjoyed the sight of his apprentice laid out naked on the bed like this. Leaning over, he gave him a quick peck on the cheek. He then traced his tongue down Duncan's spine before coming to the top of his buttocks. He took the opportunity to take a bite out of Duncan's exquisite derriere before prising him open and penetrating him with the tip of his tongue.

"Ahhh!" he groaned, not being able to control himself.

Automatically, he arched his back, rearing himself up further into Daniel's face. His flexibility made it all the better for getting fucked.

Leaning over, Daniel spat on his own throbbing cock before swiftly sliding himself into Duncan in one smooth motion.

"Fuuuuckkkk." he cried out aloud, not entirely disliking the pain.

Pinning him down by the neck, Daniel told him to shut up. Another quick slap of the arse before sliding back in fully once again. There was more groaning from Duncan as Daniel was only just beginning to work up a sweat.

He wasn't going to go easy. In fact, he wanted this to hurt. Just the way Duncan had begged for it so many times before. They were both playing out their preferred go-to roles and were loving it.

Sliding out again, he took his cock and slapped it firmly off Duncan's ass. He liked seeing his pale skin, thick, hard and strong against his lover's ebony smoothness. He could do this all night long. In bed with Duncan, he had the libido and stamina of a man half his own age.

Daniel took his cock in his hand, feeling masculine and powerful, and pulled open Duncan with his other hand. Then he edged his way in again. Enjoying the sight of being swallowed up by Duncan's warmth. Bending low, he pushed deeply. As far as he could go, he grinded himself right up into Duncan. His balls now resting heavily on Duncan's as they lay on the bed between his open legs. With his tongue, Daniel licked the edge of his ear and whispered that Duncan wasn't going to be able to walk after he'd finished with him.

"Fuck me Daniel, tell me I've been bad," he groaned.

And Daniel did.

For the next forty-five minutes, he had Duncan every which way. He had him on the bed. He fucked him in the chair. He picked Duncan up and fucked him whilst standing, both of them enjoying the view of their naked bodies all hot and entwined in the full-length mirror. At one point they'd ended up on the floor, but were still going for it as if they hadn't noticed.

Afterwards, keen to wash the sex and sweat off, they shared a shower. Not being able to resist, Daniel fucked his employee in there, too.

By eleven, they were both spent. There was nothing left and neither one of them could manage any more sex. For now, at least...

The plan was always to go back to work.

The whole point of getting the hotel room was that Daniel was supposed to go back and spend a few hours more in the workshop. There was so much still to be done there.

But then, Duncan was *supposed* to have gone home and Daniel was supposed to have gone back to Aiken's house for the night before starting over again tomorrow and the next day.

Instead, they fell asleep together for the first time as a couple, in a king-sized hotel bed made for secret rendezvous just like the one they were having.

Waking again a few hours later, Daniel fucked him all over again.

The Previous Wednesday

Eight

Aiken hadn't slept well all night. Thoughts about his business and his tenancy agreement, along with hiding so much from Billy, prevented him from getting much sleep at all. At least Billy hadn't been hanging around the house to ask questions like he normally did. Because Aiken was a terrible liar and Billy always saw right through them. There was also Broderick sticking his nose in, trying to cash in on his temporary financial problems. Up until recently, he'd never questioned his life choices, but now, in hindsight, would he have been better off going into business with Broderick right from the start?

Aiken was hopeful, though. He knew how easy it would be to sort everything out. How quickly he could fix every little thing that had gone wrong, all with Billy being none the wiser. One last flutter and all of his problems would be resolved for good. He'd certainly learnt his lesson and after getting himself out of a hole he promised himself that he was done with gambling for good.

Excited about the days ahead, and that all important race on Friday, he let his mind run away from him on what could be.

Last night he'd received a quick courtesy text from Daniel telling him he probably wouldn't make it back for supper again. That he'd probably end up getting a take-way and working as late as possible in the workshop. Daniel had promised not to wake him up when he came in, or when he left again first thing the next morning.

Regardless of what Daniel had said, Aiken knew he hadn't come home at all. Tossing and turning all night, and usually a light sleeper at the best of times, Aiken would have heard the front door go, either last night or this morning. And that just didn't happen.

Although it was none of his business, he did wonder where Daniel had got to last night and why he hadn't just said he was staying at the workshop.

Aiken didn't mind too much, after all, it's not like he owed him anything. Although, he had to admit, he enjoyed spending time with him over breakfast yesterday. Billy rarely got up to see Aiken off during the week, so it was nice to have some company. It was also refreshing to talk about proper things. Meaningful things. And with Daniel also being a businessman, they definitely had a bit more in common on that front too. They'd both worked hard to build up their reputations. They both had shops, employees and a brand name to uphold.

Maybe Billy and James were onto something when they joked the couples would have been better off from the start, swapped as they were this week. Although Aiken had little sexual interest in Daniel, regardless of how typically hand-some he was or how well he'd maintained (and liked to subtly show off) his physique. Aiken's sex drive was pretty low anyway, but Daniel and his arrogance didn't do anything for him; Aiken would always prefer what he had with his own loving husband.

Aiken could have done with someone to talk to this morn-ing, actually. He couldn't talk to Billy about it, there was no way of talking to Silvie, or God forbid - Broderick, but maybe Daniel, with all the same stresses as running a business could understand the things that were troubling him, and what to do, if anything, about Broderick's offer.

***

James and Billy had another relaxing work-free day ahead of them. This morning, they were enjoying their pastries, drinking coffee, and playing with Cleo. He was loving all of the extra attention, and so far, hadn't seemed to notice that his Papa was missing at all which said far more about Daniel than it did their son

James had noticed that without Daniel rushing around, huffing at the mess, or complaining about something or other, there was a much calmer ambiance to the kitchen. Everyone was smiling, no one was stressing out. It was re-freshing, and the placidity seemed to be rubbing off on Cleo, too.

Although James was looking forward to an afternoon on

the beach, he was actually quite content where he was right now. It was all very domesticated and homely. Both of them appreciated the company on what otherwise would have been them sitting alone in their own homes at this time of the morning. If he hadn't have promised himself to at least do *something* this week with Billy, then he may have just given into laziness and stayed home all afternoon in the garden.

"I could get used to this," Billy said, shovelling food into Cleo's mouth via an aeroplane spoon.

He was sitting in the highchair at the end of the kitchen table. Most of the porridge had ended up on his bib, the floor, or Billy himself, but it was all good. He was a hungry little boy and just a tad overexcited to be having his breakfast.

"With the amount you're doing around here with Cleo, so could I," he smiled, meaning it completely.

Billy's phone pinged; a text message.

"Hey, what's the betting it's not from my husband? He never texts me."

"Right! Mine neither. Glad it's not just me then," James replied, thinking about the shower door again.

"Oh, it's from Dana, actually."

He read the message, furrowing his brow.

"Everything okay? She hasn't pulled out, has she?" James asked, getting a little nervous for his friend. He knew it was all too good to be true.

The couple had been waiting nearly a year already for adoption. This did kind of feel like it was all too easy, and that it all seemed to be happening so quickly. It was only a week or two ago that Billy had been contacted by her. And they'd only met on Monday. So much could go wrong, and James just wanted his friend to take it slowly. Above all, he wanted to protect him from getting overexcited and then ultimately let down.

"No, nothing like that. She said she wants to stick around town a little longer. Get to know me properly and then meet Aiken before we 'do' anything."

"That's good, isn't it?" James presumed.

"Yeah. Course it is. Dana's a pro at this. She's done surrogacy four times before. She knows exactly what she's doing. She's even provided me a list of references, other gay and straight parents that she's had babies for. It's all above board. Totally legit."

"What's the problem, then?"

"Nothing."

"Go on. I can tell when there's something up. You're not bouncing up and down like you usually do."

"Well..." he sighed. "You don't actually *pay* for surrogacy in the UK as it's against the law... And quite frankly we wouldn't want to 'buy' a baby if that was the case, anyway. But we are expected to pay for the cost of doing it, which obviously includes 'reasonable living expenses'," he said using air quotes.

"And what, she's asked for unreasonable expenses?"

"No, not at all. She hasn't asked for any money or anything like that. But I did pay her money for her travel, and for her hotel whilst she's in town. It's just that if she stays longer, I'll need to give her some more. I've paid myself so far, with it all being a surprise for Aiken. And I haven't got much left in my account, that's all. If she stays longer than a day or two, I might need a word with him, you know, and that would totally spoil the surprise for him before I'm ready."

"I can lend you some if it helps," James offered without hesitation. "Daniel likes to brag about how much money he makes. Let's see him put it to good use for a change!"

"Thanks, but it's fine. I'll see how I get on with her over the next couple of days, and then I suppose she'll have to meet him, anyway. It's all good. I guess I'm just getting nervous about it. It was all a great idea for so long and now it's actually happening I think the reality of it all is setting in."

"You're not getting cold feet, are you?"

"God no. Nothing like that. It's just actually happening now. It's so exciting, but obviously a little daunting."

"I know that feeling. Kinda like when the adoption agency called us and said that they had 'a prospective match', which then turned out to be Cleo."

James could see that Billy was buzzing. It was all getting a little much for him. It was understandable, under the circumstances, especially as he didn't have his husband yet onboard with the plan. That in itself was enough to make Billy edgy; after all, most of the couple's admin, arranging, and big decisions were usually taken care of by Aiken. Billy didn't even know how to change a tyre, or even call for the AA without his husband, so he was obviously going to find going solo on this challenging to begin with.

"Ah, that'll be the postman," James said, jumping off his stool at the noise of the bell.

Leaving him to finish off with Cleo, he wondered about Billy's predicament. He didn't want to say it, but he really was a little nervous for his best friend. How much did he actually know about surrogacy, or this Dana girl who just happened to pop up out of the blue? He also had a sneaky suspicion that Aiken wouldn't be up for it in the same way as Billy, once he found out, which would be a whole other problem in itself. What was Billy going to do if Aiken put his foot down and said no? He'd be absolutely devastated.

Pushing his concerns aside, he answered the door.

The sun caught his eye as it dazzled in brightness. It was going to be another scorcher and perfect weather for the beach.

"Oh, Shirley. It's you," he said, sounding surprised.

He certainly wasn't expecting to see her this early. Shirley never called around at this time, and when she did, it was usually to complain. He was going to be in for an earful for one thing or other.

"Here," she said, ignoring pleasantries. She shoved something into his hand. "I don't appreciate having to come around to deliver your post."

"Sorry Shirley. I was in, but didn't hear the doorbell go until just now. It's not my fault the postman got it wrong."

"It's the third time this month. You need to speak to them. I'm sick of having to deliver things for you like this."

"Maybe the postman has a thing for you?" James joked before remembering who he was talking to.

She was *not* impressed. Without another word, she turned on her heels and left him stood there on the front doorstep in his pyjamas and dressing down.

"Thank you!" he shouted to the back of her head as she stormed off.

Cleo had finished the full bowl of porridge, and Billy was doing his best to tidy up by the time James had returned to breakfast. Even with wet wipes, kitchen roll and a damp sponge, it was impossible to get him all cleaned up. "There must be a knack to this, is there?" he asked as James returned.

It seemed that in cleaning Cleo; he'd got himself just as messy.

"There is. Close your eyes and just forget about it all. Seriously, you don't have to worry about any of that. Thanks for sorting him out, though. I'll bung everything in the washer once I've got him dressed. Oh, don't let me forget, will you... I must drop this off to Daniel at work. I know he's been waiting for a couple of bits in the post, and he asked if I could," James said, pulling Cleo out for a cuddle.

"Ooh. Maybe it's a surprise present for you?" Billy suggested, intrigued, "because he misses you so much."

"I very much doubt that, as he usually forgets to even get me a valentine's card let alone a random 'I love you' gift. No, it'll be something for him, no doubt. He's been ordering loads of stuff recently. It might even be for work. It does say 'urgent' printed on it."

The box wasn't very large, smaller than a shoe box, and not very heavy. It was wrapped tightly in crisp brown paper and, on top, had their address printed in neat handwriting. Shaking the parcel gently, he could hear something rattling about inside.

"You don't fancy opening it?" Billy asked, intrigued. "I would, and then just plead ignorance afterwards."

"Not a chance. He goes mental whenever I go near his post. I've told him countless times when something's addressed to *Mr Coben* it could legitimately be mine just as much as his, but he still goes mad."

"What's he trying to hide?" Billy joked.

"Well, whatever it is, this one is very clearly addressed to *Daniel* Coben. My life wouldn't be worth living if I had a peek."

"Weird. I always open Aiken's post. I think he gets a lot sent to work anyway, but he doesn't go mad."

"Maybe your husband is far more trusting of you than mine is of me."

Billy rolled his eyes as he popped the kettle back on. Before heading off to the beach, he had to nip home to get some swimming shorts and to pick up some spare underwear for the rest of the week. He was as excited about their plans as he was about his extra time off this week.

As James had a couple of errands to run in town, including dropping off the parcel, they agreed to meet at the beach at one o'clock for some well-earned down time.

They just about had time for another coffee, maybe even another croissant or two, before they would have to get going.

As usual, both of them took far longer than they should have, and ended up rushing to get out of the house in time.

***

Kirk wasn't a bad man, he really wasn't. He had just been misunderstood his whole life.

He knew what he wanted and usually got it. It was that easy when you were as good looking as he was. Sure, he might be a little short, but lots of guys liked that, and it had certainly never stopped him getting his way before. Any guy would be lucky to have him, and he couldn't believe that James had been so rude to him when they'd met.

On his way to pick up a couple of old friends he'd already reacquainted himself with, Kirk had the windows rolled down and enjoyed the sun on his face. The heat reminded him of back home. Well, not home anymore, he figured. He was home now and back for good. That meant that unfortunately Jersey was no longer 'home'. But being on the beach on a hot day like this would feel just the same, he told himself.

The traffic was busy, even for a Wednesday. He guessed a lot of people had the same idea: Avoid the town centre, make for the seaside.

With his music blaring, he stopped at traffic lights by the

junction of The Cedar Court Inn and Coben Oak.

Coben Oak.

What are the chances of that? That's got to be Daniel's business, hasn't it?

As luck would have it, just as Kirk pulled away from the junction, the transit van with Coben Oak printed on the side pulled into the car park.

Up front was non-other than Daniel himself.

A few years older, but still as handsome as ever.

He was tempted to change course, to swing back on himself and go find a bargain in the showroom, but he was already late for his friends.

That might have to wait for another day.

Nine

"That's the first lot done," Daniel boasted as he swept in through the shop door. "Bloody hell, it's hot in here."

Duncan was unusually lethargic, but still trying his best to busy himself amongst the smaller items near the till. It was boiling inside and he had the fans going full blast. It hadn't quite done the trick, as he was still hot, and wore the slightest glow of perspiration. Daniel had been the same, and was hoping to find some relief in the shade of the shop.

"What, you've dropped them all off? Already?"

"Only for the Henderson delivery. I've got another run to make tomorrow, so long as I finish in time this evening. How's it been in here?"

"Dead in the past hour or so, I think it must be the heat. We had a few walk-ins first thing, and I've booked in a consultation for you next Monday, but other than that, it's been really quiet."

Daniel shrugged a 'no problem'.

A lot of his business was coming in online now, so a quiet morning in the shop wasn't anything to be concerned about. He reckoned that in a few years' time he could probably get away without needing the shop at all, but as it was conveniently attached to his workshop, it made sense to keep it. He loved his workshop, and the feeling of success it gave him and he wouldn't part with that for anything.

He'd been productive, at least. Most of the smaller items he was able to deliver himself in the back of his work van. Anything larger was usually delivered on a Thursday when the shop was closed to the public. On Thursdays, both he and Duncan would spend the day training and working on their orders in between the deliveries that Daniel couldn't manage on his own. It was a relief to have everything out so early, so he could spend the rest of the day focusing on what he loved most about his dream job. Creating handcrafted, self-designed bespoke pieces of *art* in his workshop.

He walked back to the large pane of glass he'd just come through and peered out. No one there. Flipping the sign, he locked the door and beckoned Duncan to follow him through to the back.

"I wanted you to take a look at this," Daniel said without looking as Duncan trailed behind.

He stopped in the middle of the workshop and turned to face his employee. Smiling, he didn't need to tell Duncan what was expected. Flies down, Daniel already had his dick in his hand, ready and waiting.

After last night and this morning, he knew how amazing it was, but it didn't stop Duncan from waiting another taste.

Without saying a word, he bent to his knees and took him in as fully as he could. Over the past two months, there'd been a lot of practice. With regular late nights, early mornings, Thursday afternoons and even last night, which had been their first (of hopefully many more to come) full night together, they'd managed to clock up a lot of time shagging together.

Although Duncan certainly wasn't new to sleeping with men, or his boss, Daniel's cock still took some getting used to.

Liking the validation of a job well done, Duncan looked up to see if Daniel approved.

The jury was still out.

"That's good, but I'm gonna need a bigger performance from you if you want that bonus. Take your clothes off," he ordered firmly.

Duncan obliged. By now, his dick was rock hard to match. He stripped, pulling his shirt over his head and, after pulling his erection out, letting his shorts and boxers fall to the floor before stepping out of them. He was already sweaty from such a hot day. With the extra heat, things were going to get really messy.

Daniel pulled himself free, sliding his opened jeans down to just below his buttocks. Pulling his tightly fitting t-shirt up, he revealed his washboard midriff, which was enough to make Duncan's cock swell. He was leaking with the first drops of sticky pre-cum, too.

Duncan backed himself up towards the workbench, and as usual, followed Daniel's lead. This time, Daniel wanted to see everything. The shine of perspiration made his dark skin look like it was glowing.

Wrapping his big hands around Duncan's small but muscular buttocks, he gently squeezed them before picking his toy-boy up. Sliding him onto the edge of the bench, he bent over to suck the tip of Duncan's big black cock.

"Hmmm." He groaned, enjoying the saltiness. "Looks like someone's turned on."

Taking his hand, he slowly slid back the foreskin to reveal the deep purple head; shiny and hard. He sucked it again, sliding down as far as he could, before coming back up for air.

No more Mr nice guy.

Daniel firmly pushed Duncan down onto the table, grabbed his thighs and slid him to the edge so that his ass was more accessible.

Another quick squeeze of Duncan's buttocks and he then lifted and pushed the underside of his thighs deep into Duncan's chest, revealing the jackpot.

Daniel idly dribbled a long trail of his saliva onto Duncan's hole, and then a little more onto his own erect cock. Rubbing it down the shaft that had already been moistened by pre-cum, he was now ready.

He slid himself into his fuck-buddy in one swift, confident motion.

"Ahhh," Duncan shouted. "Fucking hell, that's big."

Daniel grinned, "you should be used to it now, you cock-tease."

Duncan always complained that it hurt. He always shouted out at the pain, but it didn't stop him from begging for more. He loved it rough, and Daniel knew it all too well.

Building up a determined rhythm, Daniel took Duncan's erection in his hand and enjoyed playing with the skin. Sliding it up and down to reveal the full head of his impressive cock.

Outside, the croon of a seagull caught Daniel's attention. The workshop door had been left open to help encourage a non-existent draft. Daniel revelled in the element of danger, and the possibility of getting caught by a customer. Sure, he'd never actually *want* to be seen like this, but just the possibility if it was a real turn on for him. In truth, it was probably the main reason why he'd wanted to start their workplace affair in the first place.

Like Duncan, Daniel liked showing off. He also liked fucking, so the thought of doing both together was incredibly hot and far too exciting to resist.

"You didn't get enough last night?" Daniel questioned aggressively.

"God No, I want more. Give it to me," Duncan screamed, as he was getting banged so roughly.

It was lucky there were no neighbouring buildings in earshot, otherwise the police may have been called on account of all the noise.

***

Back home, due to their usual procrastination, everything

had been a mad rush to get out in time. *Same old, same old.*

Neither of them learnt. And neither of them would change...

He was just about out of the door, Cleo in tow, when he spotted the parcel. That word 'urgent' called out to him like a warning beacon. It may as well have been written in red with flashing lights. There's no way he could have ignored it, knowing how much Daniel was waiting for it and everyone knew Daniel didn't like waiting for things.

"Shit," he muttered, getting into a fluster.

He was going to be seriously late for their beach picnic if he didn't hurry up. He was already quite peckish, even after such a long-drawn-out breakfast.

Grabbing the parcel, he ran out of the door, strapped the toddler into his car seat, and was on his way as quickly as possible.

He was sweating before he'd managed to turn the air conditioning on, a mix of rushing about, and unusually high summer temperatures. Today was going to be a scorcher.

"C'mon Cleo or Papa is going to be mad that he didn't get his parcel on time."

***

"You like that?" Daniel panted in between his thrusts.

"Yeah."

"You like getting all dirty on the workbench?" He asked again.

"God yeah, give it to me."

Their two bodies were now dripping with beads of sweat. Even with the heat, Daniel wasn't taking it easy on Duncan's ass, and the workout showed on both of them like glistening diamonds.

He playfully slapped Duncan's cheek, before slipping two of his fingers into Duncan's mouth. He liked to watch Duncan suck on them, or anything else of Daniels, with those big moist lips of his. He liked to feel the warmth of his tongue, exploring his fingers as he felt the warmth of Duncan's tight ass wrapped around his cock. Ragging his head from left to right, his cock grew thicker as Duncan gagged on his hand. The groans of pleasure told Daniel he wanted more.

Daniel loved seeing him stretched out like that. Duncan was lean, his skin tightly hugging the contours of his body. The muscles he had danced and flexed as he writhed under Daniel, who was towering above him. They looked so fucking hot together, glistening in the heat like that. They would have made a killing on *OnlyFans*, had they had the inclination to start an account.

"Fucking hell," Duncan shouted again, with his legs wide and up in the air.

Daniel grabbed him by the throat for purchase and leaned in. The perspiration was streaming down his dark skin and the scent of his pheromones was getting Daniel closer.

Wrestling against the weight of Daniel, Duncan pushed up, stealing a kiss. Daniel forced him back down and slapped him across the face once more, this time a little rougher. It was a game they often played. With the feeling of Daniel's palm across his cheek, Duncan was close to coming without even touching himself. Daniel was in charge and what he wanted goes. Only after he'd had his way with Duncan was Duncan allowed to enjoy the moment for himself. It's how they both liked it, and neither of them saw any reason to change.

Everything Daniel did, did it for Duncan. His firmness, his authority, the way he fucked him mercilessly. He placed his full trust in his master, and nothing was out of bounds. With his big hard cock and muscular frame, Daniel was a fucking knockout and Duncan never got bored with being with him, or being used by him.

"I'm so close..." he murmured as Daniel reached for his shaft again.

***

"Nearly done Cleo. You'll be okay waiting in the car, two minutes I promise!" he said, pulling up on the gravel outside of the shop.

At least it hadn't taken long for the aircon to kick in. It might have been boiling in the sun, but inside the car, it was practically freezing.

Usually a bit of a klutz, he made sure he'd put the hand-brake on, and turned the ignition off. He grabbed the parcel and even remembered to wind down all the windows before taking the key out. *Just in case.* There was no way he was going to let the car roll off anywhere, or get locked out with the keys still inside with the baby on a hot day like today, even if it was like a fridge in there.

It was literally two minutes.

"Daniel probably wouldn't even be in," he mumbled to himself, as if to justify leaving Cleo where he was.

He tried the front door, but it was locked.

Huh. That's odd for this time. Shouldn't that fit apprentice, Duncan be here, at least? He peered through the glass, but couldn't see anyone. He rattled the door again as if to double check, but it wouldn't open. Not wanting to leave the parcel on the step for anyone driving past to pick up, he walked around the side of the unit to try the back door. If that was locked, at least he could leave it there, out of sight, and maybe send a text to just let Daniel know it was waiting for him.

The sun was at its highest now, and he was already struggling with the heat. Not always one for sunbathing, the beach trip might have been a bad idea on such a hot day after all. At least Cleo, all sun-creamed up, would like playing in the sand and paddling in the sea.

"Daniel?" He shouted.

They weren't far from the main road. The buzz of cars, the birds chirping and the distant laughter of children that were no longer prisoners of school made it hard to hear any kind of response.

Crunching on the gravel, he made his way to the back. The workshop door was open. At least he could leave it inside if no one was about.

"Fuck, yeah... I'm coming!" a voice from within panted heavily.

And then he saw them.

Billy couldn't move. In shock, he was glued to the spot in utter disbelief.

He couldn't quite figure out what he was looking at, at first, but he absolutely knew right off the bat that it was wrong. It took a moment to sink in, but right there in front of him, he saw Daniel's shiny white ass as he held his assistant's legs wide up in the air. Without saying a word, he dropped the parcel and ran back to the car as quickly as he could.

"Fuck! Fucking hell, who was that?" Daniel squirmed, pulling out of Duncan as swiftly as he could. Struggling to yank his chinos up over his sweaty legs, he fell over. Panicking now, he wrestled to pull his clothes in order. Getting up, he stumbled to the back door to see what had been dropped, desperate to catch a glimpse of who had caught them in the act.

***

James had completed his errands in town early. Not having Cleo with him allowed him to finish much quicker than expected. So early, in fact, that he had the perfect opportunity to go and see his husband for a quick coffee just before lunch. Maybe, as they'd not seen each other in a few days, they might even get some time for a bit of... eh, who was

James kidding?

He was *almost* certain that Daniel would never do that at work.

At least he had a fun afternoon at the beach to look forward to afterwards.

In his own little world, he hadn't noticed Billy and Cleo frantically pass him as he pulled into the otherwise empty carpark of *Coben Oak*.

Excited to see his husband, he yanked at the front door but it wouldn't budge.

"Daniel... Daniel?" he shouted, before walking around to the back.

James knew that his husband took every chance he got to work outside during the summer months. He'd often be found with the back door wide open and his radio on, busily sanding this, or oiling that. He might even be out in the sun with his shirt off, *fingers crossed*, looking all hot and muscly as he worked on his furniture and his tan.

Inside, Daniel was frantically trying to straighten himself up when he heard someone calling out.

"Are you there, Daniel?"

Shit. Fucking hell, thought Daniel, *that can't have been James that caught us, surely?*

"James?" he shouted as calmly as he could. "Hang on a sec!"

Jogging around the side of the building, he was desperate to intercept his husband before it was too late. He had to stop him from coming inside and finding Duncan in whatever questionable state of undress he was currently in.

"Hey honey, thought I'd pop in and say hi. You're all sweaty? Are you okay?" he asked, going in for a kiss.

"Uh, fine yeah. Just lugging a big piece of furniture about, that's all. Heavy work in this heat. I'm absolutely knackered," he panted.

"Where's Duncan? The shop door is closed and there's a sign up saying you're closed."

"Huh, that's odd. Let's go have a look?"

Shit. How was he going to explain this? At least if he hadn't been caught, he could say Duncan had locked up for an emergency. He had to nip out somewhere, or maybe he was at an early lunch, but an excuse like that wouldn't work if James knew that he was there.

Just as they made their way around the front, Duncan, *now fully clothed,* was just propping the door open.

"Hey James, how are you?" he asked sheepishly and rather flushed.

"Good, thanks. Thought I'd come check to see if my husband was working hard. You've just reopened?"

"Err. No, I think the door was just sticking in the heat. I've propped it open now to let a bit of a draft in," he lied, hoping it had done the trick.

"Ah. Yeah, you look pretty hot, too. It must be stifling in there; I don't know how you manage," James said, brushing it off.

Daniel cast an eye over to Duncan, and grateful for his quick thinking. Heaving a sigh of relief, he led his husband back around to the workshop and away from his secret lover.

No matter how much he liked his afternoon delight, he couldn't chance anything like this again at work.

Ten

Fucking hell.

Fuck.

What am I going to tell James? It will break his heart.

Why did I have to go and see a thing like that?

So much for helping Daniel out with his parcel!

There's Cleo to think about, too...

Suddenly, Billy wasn't looking forward to an afternoon on the beach at all. As a matter of fact, he wasn't looking forward to seeing James at all. He was just so glad that it was him that had taken the parcel to the workshop, and that he had left Cleo in the car when he did. It would have been unforgivable if Daniel's own son had walked in on him shagging Duncan, asking what Papa was doing to that strange man.

Thank God I'd left him in the car.

Panicking and without any idea of what to do, Billy had phoned Aiken. He wanted to see him, to ask his advice on how to handle things. He only needed to pop in for a minute. But as usual, he'd had the stock response; 'too busy, we'll chat later', but where did that leave Billy?

Somehow, over the last few years, he'd realised that later never actually came. The one time he really needed advice from his husband, and he wasn't even there for that.

His bad mood had quickly turned into a foul one.

Not wanting to let James down, or let him know that something was wrong, he'd decided he had to meet him at the beach regardless of how much he now detested the idea. He would go, and just pretend that everything was okay. At least it could buy him some time before making any rash decisions.

Fucking hell, what a mess.

And what a bastard Daniel was for doing that in the first place.

***

The afternoon sun was relentless, beating down on them as though the summer would never end. There was the laughter of children from every direction and the sound of several different kinds of music flowing across the beach, which almost made them feel like they were on a foreign holiday. Somewhere hot, but still very British.

It should have been a fantastic afternoon at the seaside.

They were all prepared, with sun-cream, the parasols out and a little pop-up tent for Cleo to play in, or sleep should he need a nap.

Everything was set for a great afternoon of doing nothing, but James could tell there was something hanging in the air between them.

"What's up? Billy, what's up? Are you okay?" James asked again with a touch of concern just creeping into his voice.

"No, it's fine. I mean. I'm fine. Nothing's up. I'm fine. How are you?" he asked absentmindedly.

"I'm good, thank you. I wasn't asking in general. You seem a bit off this afternoon. Has something happened? You look distracted. Do you wanna go home or something?" he asked, trying to wrack his brains over what it could be. "Are you missing Aiken?"

Billy usually wore his heart on his sleeve and would tell James everything, no matter how insignificant. Keeping something bottled up, especially something so huge, wasn't like him at all. Billy knew he'd been quiet ever since meeting up on the beach. He'd barely touched their picnic, which was unheard of for Billy. He'd tried to appear normal, his usual aloof self, but it was easier said than done.

At least Cleo was pleased to see him. He was playing with his big yellow digger truck in the sand and having an absolute blast. There was a family not too far away, and their son, a little older than Cleo, was seemingly working up the courage to ask if he wanted to play. Kids at that age were so cute to watch, right before the inevitable shyness set in. Kids that age had no idea of the traumas that came along in later life.

Maybe James could take him for a quick paddle before they came back and had seconds. Maybe after a quick swim his friend would have cheered up a bit too, hopefully.

"Fancy a dip?" he asked Billy hopefully.

"No, you go. I'll watch Cleo if he doesn't want to join you. Have fun."

Billy couldn't bear to see James like this. Acting as though there was nothing wrong. Well, as far as he was concerned, there wasn't, Billy supposed.

But one way or another, his – and Cleo's – lives were about to be turned upside down, no doubt.

Tell him, or not tell him?

Was it even his place to? He couldn't carry on for long, as though nothing had changed, that was for sure. Keeping it from his best friend was already tearing him up inside and he'd only known about it a couple of hours.

Maybe he could confront Daniel himself. Get to the bottom of it all. Maybe there was an innocent explanation... well, with a position like that it couldn't be totally innocent, but it might have just been a one off, never to be repeated again?

That wouldn't be right, though. Although he wanted to protect his friend, he didn't want to step on his toes and take control over a situation that really was none of his business. Either way, he was stuck between a rock and a hard place.

Billy watched James trot off down to the shoreline in the blazing afternoon heat. He could see the sparking whiteness dance on top of the rippling surface and wondered how warm the water would really be. Even on a summer's day like this, he'd never once felt the sea that lapped up against the English shoreline 'warm'. It didn't stop people from pretending though, did it? Maybe that's what he needed to do.

Billy couldn't understand why Daniel would need or want to cheat on his best friend like that. Yes, he'd put on a little weight since hitting his thirties, but that was normal, expected, even. He was six foot four, of course he needed to fill out a bit. Who wants to sleep with a lanky guy at that age, anyway? In fact, he would have looked better with a bit of weight on when he was younger, to be honest, but ultimately that shouldn't matter. They were married, and supposedly in love. You don't care if you're husband puts a bit of weight on if you're really in love with them.

Although it might pain him to admit it under normal circumstances, James had always been a good-looking guy. A fantastic dad to Cleo, a loyal friend and really good fun to boot. He'd always made Billy laugh, other than today, maybe, but that definitely wasn't James' fault. He was just an all-around great catch. In fact, James had been Billy's first crush, even before he'd actually come out. That was all under the bridge now, though.

Over the years, Billy had thought that Daniel and James had made a little bit of a miss-match in one another, but that's only because he valued what James had to offer way more than what James' muscular but rather soulless husband had going for him. Billy wasn't impressed by fancy titles or career reputations, either. It was the person that count, not the bank balance, after all.

He glanced over at Cleo, who was now occupied by the other boy. Between them, they were trying to build a sandcastle, but failing miserably. Neither of them seemed to mind, however, and continued babbling, laughing and trying to talk to one another.

Billy closed his eyes and rolled over. Even the tingling heat on his back didn't allow him to forget the awful predicament he was in.

Why did I have to go and walk in on them like that? I was only trying to do Daniel a favour in the first place, and this is how it turned out.

Running straight in, the sea felt beautifully refreshing on such a hot day. James certainly couldn't have gone for a swim like this if Billy hadn't been around this week. There was no chance Daniel would have taken a couple of hours out to either come down with him or keep an eye on Cleo in the showroom. He didn't even seem happy to see him when he popped in earlier for some reason, for that matter. After so many years together, it wasn't really a surprise, though.

James briefly pondered if Duncan would mind keeping an eye on him in the shop, just to give him a little break for an hour, but then quickly realised it was a preposterous idea. He was sure Duncan wouldn't mind – he always seemed happy to see the little guy, but he knew Daniel wouldn't allow it. He'd bark on about professionalism and needing to get work done. 'This is *your* full-time job' he'd say, not appreciating, or caring that he never actually got a break from his 'job' like Daniel did.

Looking back towards the sand, he smiled at the sight of Cleo making friends with the other kid. James was so proud of his little boy. He may overcompensate now with cracking jokes or being outwardly confident, but in reality, he'd been a very shy child at a young age, finding it difficult to make friends. When he made one in Billy, he'd done everything to successfully maintain it. Laid out like that in the full sun, James couldn't help but wonder if Billy had put enough cream on. He was known for being a little careless with his own health, but he'd certainly regret it later if he hadn't.

There was something definitely up with him today. James had known him too well and too long to believe that everything was fine.

Maybe it was something with Aiken. He knew Billy was missing him, but this seemed bigger than that. He would usually be the first to tell James what was up, especially if it was relationship stuff, but today, for some reason he'd decided to keep it all bottled up. He'd never known Billy be so quiet and it unnerved him.

James dunked his head under the water and began to swim. Formulating plans, he wondered what he could do tonight that was both fun and would also take Billy's mind off whatever it was that was bothering him. He didn't want to have to resort to another bottle of wine and another throwaway film, but if nothing better came to mind, it might have to do.

Back on the beach, and Billy was half asleep. With his eyes closed, he tried to think of happier times. Laughter and fun, when having husbands was the reason you were happy, not the reason your life could be ruined with one 'I have something to tell you' conversation.

Not far away, he could hear the constant but reassuring babble of Cleo trying to have a chat with the other boy. It was sweet. They seemed to understand one another, to some extent at least. And then, from above, Billy was distracted by a familiar and rather unpleasant voice.

"Hello there, stranger."

Billy squinted to see who was talking and if they were even talking to him or not.

Oh dear. Well, today has just gone from bad to worse.

Billy sat up and automatically sucked in his tummy as best as possible. Immediately self-conscious about being laid out in nothing but his beach shorts.

It was Kirk. Perfectly proportioned Kirk, in the tightest, skimpiest speedos. Clearly working on his tan and probably trying to stir some trouble, as usual.

"Kirk. James said you were back," he reluctantly said, not really wanting to get into a conversation.

"I guess he must have been excited to see me then, talking about me to everyone like that... he hasn't called me yet, though. I was expecting an invite for drinks already," he laughed.

"I thought we'd seen the last of you years ago. Who are you with, anyway?" Billy asked, looking around and ignoring Kirk's cynicism.

"A couple of gal friends. So seriously, when are we all going to catch up?"

"We're very busy."

"You don't have to be so mean, Billy. I was trying to be friendly. You know, maybe you could take a lesson in it."

"Well, you are known for being friendly, Kirk," he said sarcastically, before mumbling, "that and trying to wreck people's relationships."

"Hey, I heard that, and it's not fair–"

"Look Kirk. Why are you hanging around all of a sudden? It's not like we all stayed in touch. It's not like we're *friends*. What are you after?"

"All of that is in the past. It was a lifetime ago and I've grown up. I genuinely want to catch up with you all. I've missed you," he said, before changing his tone. "How's Daniel doing, anyway? I saw something online about his business. It looks like it's really taken off now. He must be doing really well for himself?"

"Yep."

Kirk paused. As if waiting for more. With a smile on his face, he was about to say something, but stopped himself. Another pause and then he went on. "Well, it would be nice to see him. I'd love to catch up with him properly..."

Billy just stared at him, slowly raising an eyebrow.

"Oh, don't look like that. Of course I meant you too... you and James *and* Daniel. It'll be like old times," he grinned smugly.

"That's what I'm afraid of."

Billy was keen to get rid of Kirk before James returned. He already felt bad about what he'd seen earlier at the workshop. James having to deal with Kirk too would make things even worse. This week was quickly turning into the worst week of their lives and it was only Wednesday lunchtime!

Thinking of no better way to close their conversation, Billy lied and promised he'd get James to set something up soon. He then rolled over and closed his eyes before waiting for Kirk to say anything else.

He just wanted him gone. Away from them on the beach and out of his life for good, but that seemed easier said than done.

Billy mused over what James had alluded to regarding Kirk. Kirk had certainly tried to split Daniel and James up right before they were married, and it was definitely something Kirk would do for kicks if for no other reason. But reading between the lines now, he didn't get the impression that Kirk was after James so much, no. There was a strong chance he hadn't turned over the new leaf he was claiming to have, and he may want to get between the couple again. But from how Billy understood it, it seemed that Kirk was now after Daniel instead.

***

Later that night, James had insisted on Billy getting "dressed up", which actually only meant putting a shirt on instead of lounging around in his pyjamas again. He hadn't told Billy what he had planned. That bit would be a surprise, a nice one, hopefully. He promised it wasn't a big deal, but that it should put a smile on his face, at least.

Cleo was fed, bathed, read to and tucked up in bed by seven on the dot. With both men sharing the responsibility, Cleo was having the time of his life and Billy was getting in the much-needed practice.

Exhausted after such a draining day (not to mention a mild case of sunburn) Billy had half a mind to cancel James' plans and head straight to bed when Cleo did. There was no stopping James, though, who'd promised the evening would be well worth it.

Reluctantly, which was saying something for Billy, they had poured their first Bacardi's by seven thirty and at five to eight, there was a loud knock on the front door. Not being able to hold back his grin, James insisted that Billy answered it.

"Oh, is it a fireman stripper just for me?" He asked deadpan, but secretly thinking that the sight of a well-toned, semi-naked, hopefully oiled-up hunk might actually cheer him up a little bit even if he could only look and not touch.

"Oh my God, Penny!" Billy screamed with a huge smile exploding across his face.

This was not what he was expecting at all, but was far better than a man in a uniform.

"Jessica. Oh, my God, you're both back!" he added, almost in tears.

Giving them both a massive hug, he was genuinely over the moon to see them, and had, for now at least, forgotten all about James' problems and the reason why he was so upset in the first place.

Knowing Billy as he did, clearly James understood exactly what was needed to cheer him up and had pulled it off perfectly.

Penny had been Billy's fag-hag, closest-girlfriend and second-best-friend for almost as long as he had known James. Jessica was Penny's best friend, and they were all close to James, too. The girls had been travelling around south America for the last six months. They had been expected back in about two or three weeks, so this really was a shock. Not that he was complaining about it now they were here.

"How did you manage this?" he grinned at James as the three of them greeted him in the lounge.

"Oh, you know... I pulled some strings, brought in some favours... made some magic happen. The usual," he smiled, glad that it seemed to have done the trick.

He wasn't going to let Billy know it was completely co-incidental, and he'd not actually done anything other than keeping it a surprise for a couple of hours.

"Right, ladies..." Penny said to the boys. "We've brought far too much booze, a few crappy chick-flicks, some fun games and more chocolate that even you two could get through in a lifetime. You ready to have some fun?"

"Duh, have you not heard of Netflix?" James scoffed playfully. Penny gave him a whack on the shoulder in response. "I'm not that old, you sarky queen."

"That's it, I'm getting into my onesie." Billy shouted, instantly running upstairs to get changed into something more comfortable.

"Oh my God, I'm so glad you're back," James said, hugging them both. "He's been in a funk all day. He won't talk to me about it and I have no idea what's up, but I'm sure seeing you will do the trick."

"Where's Daniel, working late again?" Jessica asked, looking around.

"He's not ran off with Aiken, has he?" Penny chipped in, laughing.

"We have so much to tell you…"

The night had got off to a great, yet rather loud, start. James would have been worried about Cleo waking up, but with all the alcohol, he'd become a little lax with his otherwise quiet inside voice. The sensible parent in him had long since checked out for the evening. It probably wouldn't be long before Shirley next door would be banging on the wall, or even calling around to tell them off in person. She always had somewhere to go the following morning, or at least that was her usual excuse, the old bag. Why not just say she didn't like to even hear them breathe, which was the real truth of it?

Its' not like they had loud music on, but Billy's volume tended to rise with his excitement, and he was clearly having a blast with the girls this evening. James couldn't ask him to quieten down now, not after how sad he'd been earlier.

They'd just watched Mean Girls, and someone had decided it was time to at least try and play one of the games they'd brought with them.

"You sure that *Twister* is a good idea?" James pondered,

whilst trying to step over to the mat.

"Of course it is. It's the perfect time to play," Jessica piped up, happily sat back in the armchair after making the executive decision to spin, rather than partake herself. "This game is made for drinking."

Before long, Penny had collapsed and therefore lost, and somehow Billy had his crotch stuffed right in James' face. There might have been a grimace, but he was concentrating hard on not falling over. Billy would never let him live it down.

"I'd watch what you're doing there Bil," Jessica laughed. "We all know what James' sex drive is like and without his husband around... well, who knows what he might try to take a bite out of?"

James looked up, grinned, and pretended to go for it. After his sordid dream, she might have been on to something there.

Billy couldn't hold back any longer. Doubling over in a fit of hysterics, his genitalia, visibly loose and hanging – without underwear – in his onesie, collapsed down onto James.

As James muffled something to Billy about getting his dick out of his mouth, the rest of them burst out laughing.

"Right. Another round of drinks and then let's play something else." Penny grinned excitedly.

"Whatever did you have in mind?" James asked curiously. He was tipsy enough to be up for almost anything now, just as the rest of them were.

Penny reached across the coffee table, grabbed an empty bottle of wine (fortunately a closed screw-top) and dangled it seductively.

"You have got to be joking me!" Billy screamed. "Not a chance."

"Not even after getting us tanked up," James agreed.

"C'mon, it's just a laugh," she pushed. "I'm dying for some manly contact, and since there's no chance of that tonight, you two will have to do."

"Didn't you get any action with the natives?" Billy asked. "I thought you'd be totally shagged out with all those hot Brazilians with fiery temperaments and huge dicks."

"Fat chance. There were more pasty-looking ginger guys than you could throw a stick at. It was like being at a secondary school scout retreat for most of the trip. They just seemed to follow us everywhere. I'm gagging for a *decent* shag."

"Don't look at us! You two ladies might be 'young'," he laughed, "free, and single, but we are both happily married." James said authoritatively.

Even if he was single, the thought of snogging Penny was a bit much. Especially after the amount of booze both of them had consumed. It would only end in tears, or maybe a bit of vomit.

"Don't talk crap," Penny slurred, on her way back from the loo. "You know it doesn't – hic – count if you're kissing girls. C'mon, it'll be a laugh. She doesn't really want to shag either of you, she's not that desperate. There was at least one nerdy looking back-packer that I'm pretty sure gave her a pity-fuck... or was it the other way round, Pen?"

She wisely chose not to answer.

The four of them fell down to the floor, and Penny wasted no time in spinning the bottle. Before it had even stopped, she'd jumped on Billy's lap and started kissing him everywhere. His face, his head... she was over him like a bad rash, laughing and having fun.

Billy just sat there rolling his eyes, taking it like the (gay) man that he was.

Next it was his turn and with the slightest enthusiasm, he span the bottle.

Inevitably, it landed on James.

He leant in just as James mirrored him. They held their pose for a moment. Billy opened his mouth just a touch. James drew in and slowly slid his tongue out. The girls leaned in, mouths agog, excited to watch their two friends get down to it after twenty years... just before they embraced, in unison, they both turned to the girls and said "Nahh."

"Spoilsports. We wanted man on man action!" Penny laughed.

"That's enough soft-core for you two. Let's put another film on and talk all the way through it again." Billy suggested, getting up to sort out the DVD player.

"Put one of your pornos on!" Jessica suggested at the mere mention of it.

They all ignored her. There was no chance James was going to share with anyone the type of porn he jacked off to. They would probably never speak to him again, and quite rightly, too.

Billy pulled James up, cheekily slapped his arse and then picked up the remote before assisting the girls off the floor.

By the end of the second film, it was time for Penny and Jessica to go. Everyone was feeling tired, tipsy, but very happy to have spent some time back together.

They ordered a taxi and finished the last of their bottle. Conversation was far more subdued now that it had been at the beginning of the evening.

James stood up to see the girls off, his drunkenness only hitting him in full force with the rush of blood to his head. They left Billy half asleep on the couch and said their good-byes on the doorstep.

"Seems fineeeee to meeee," Penny slurred, referring to Billy's earlier mood.

"Seeya hun. C'mon yer old bag. Taxi's waiting," Jessica added.

James waved them off and returned to the living room. He was going to tidy around, but he could barely stand.

Instead, he pulled Billy off the couch and dragged him to bed. Banging off the walls, the banister and a painful doorhandle, they'd managed to make it to the first floor and had stumbled into the open door.

"You wanna brush your teeth?" he asked Billy.

"Nah. I feel a little ill."

"You wanna hand getting to bed?"

"Cheeky." *Hic.*

"I meant... never mind..." James said, playfully pushing Billy and giggling.

"Aww, I love you, James. You're the best. My best friend... but shusssh, don't tell Aiken I said – hic – that."

"You're drunk."

"So'r you. But I mean it. What would I do without you?"

Absentmindedly, James stripped to his pants, turned the light off, and got into bed.

Billy unzipped his onesie and followed him.

***

The two men slept side by side without a hint of 'will-they, won't-they' sexual desire.

Unconscious of where he was, or who he was with, Billy wrapped his arms around James and spooned his best friend. It was all above board and platonic. Two friends who had loved each other like brothers for years. Billy kissed James once on the shoulder and whispered he loved him.

James, asleep as soon as he got into bed, pushed himself into the warmth and comfort of Billy. "Hmm" He groaned, instinctively. Oblivious to being so close to someone other than his husband.

If he hadn't been so drunk, or so tired, he may have felt Billy's hard cock pressing into his buttock.

And if he'd have known what his husband had been caught doing, he may have even backed up onto Billy's dick willingly.

The Previous Thursday

It was the following morning, and the curtains had remained unclosed from the previous night. The sunlight beamed through, highlighting the tiny dust particles that danced and swirled in the slight breeze that came from the open window. Even with a little bit of circulation, the room smelled of men; hot bodies, alcohol, and other unpleasant aromas best left undetermined.

There was snoring. A cough and a splutter, and then all of a sudden Billy jumped out of bed.

"Shit. I've done it again!" he shouted before then screaming, "SHIT!" as he banged his foot on one of the dumbbells on the floor.

"Oh my God, what is it?" James said groggily, blocking out the sunlight with his hand. He rolled over and added. "What's up? Hey, you're naked, and oh my God Billy, put some pants on, you have a boner... oh my God, OH MY GOD! My eyes! Err, why are you even in my bed?"

"Fuck," he blustered, throwing his hands over his crotch. "I'm late for work. It's gone eight o'clock."

He was too hungover and too late to be embarrassed about his manhood, or to spend time trying to figure out why he was even there in the first place.

To be fair, James also had morning wood, totally unconscious and definitely not sexual, but at least he was in his own bed *and* he still had his pants on.

Why hadn't Cleo woken them up yet, asking for his breakfast?

He painfully rolled back around and picked up the alarm

clock.

"The one time you're early and you panic. It's only eight minutes past six, you dumbass. Did you pick your phone up upside down again? Are you coming back to bed for an hour, or what, because I'm not getting out until that kid drags me out?" James said with a groan, throwing his head back into the pillow. "Just do me a favour and keep that thing away from me."

***

It was a miracle. Billy had actually arrived at work early. Who knew that such a thing was even possible? Especially after an impromptu party like that. He actually thought it might be the very first time he'd been awake and out of bed at six in the morning before.

He'd opted to go back into his 'own' bed for the remainder of his lie in. No sense in getting clothes on to go back for a couple of hours' sleep, just before James was inevitably going to wake him up tending to Cleo. He had no problem sharing a bed with his best friend. They'd done it many times over the years. But the thought of willingly doing it naked was a bit much, especially when he still felt queasy from all that booze last night. Bloody hell, those girls were a bad influence. Some things don't change.

What a week, and it was only Thursday! He still couldn't believe James had now finally seen his dick. After all this time...

He'd known right from the start, right when they were teenagers, that James had fancied him. James had been interested in him before either of them knew what gay meant. He never actually said anything, but it was apparent all the same, to Billy at least.

When James came out, it took another year for Billy to realise *and admit* that he was gay too. By then, James had already been around the block a few times and was too experienced for someone struggling his way out of the closest. Billy would have been interested back then, *was* interested, in all honesty, but he didn't want to become another notch on James' bedpost. After years of knowing each other as kids, their friendship was too important to Billy to waste on a one-night stand, or even a juvenile relationship, when they were too young to actually know what they wanted out of life and out of each other.

Older and wiser, neither of them regretted choosing instead to focus on a lifelong friendship, and that's exactly what they had now. The best friendship either of them could have asked for. He might have missed out on falling in love with his best friend, but at least he hadn't lost his closest friend.

Well, *tit-for-tat*, he supposed. James had finally seen him completely naked, and with a boner, to boot. It only seemed fair, after Billy had accidentally walked in on James in the shower on Monday morning. That was rather a pleasant surprise, if you could call it that. *Who knew James was packing!*

His head was still a little sore on the drive to work. Those extra hours in bed helped, but didn't completely fix his hangover.

What a great night, though! It was fun to see the girls. He was so excited they were finally back. He knew they'd have lots more nights like that in the coming weeks.

It must have been a wild one because he couldn't for the life of him think what had happened for him to wake up next to James, in bed, *naked.*

They hadn't done anything stupid, had they?

No, of course not?

Surely he would remember if they had?

Although, thinking back, he had to admit it was nice and cosy cuddling into James like that. That little extra padding between the two of them really made for a comfortable snooze. Aiken was just a bit too thin, a bit too bony to hug well, but James had always had the knack (and the extra pound or two) to do it properly.

There was a slight breeze in the morning air as he walked from the car to work. It was a refreshing break from the summer heat that the nation was struggling to cope with. The 'hottest in however many years', 'absolute undeniable proof of global warning' and whatever else the news was telling the public, as if it would make them feel better about melting in the unnatural temperatures.

"Wow, you look rough!" Tony said as Billy let himself in.

They were good friends, and Billy always shared his latest antics with Tony as he did with Sandie. Although so much had happened in the last week, he just couldn't bring himself to repeat most of it.

After such a fun night, he couldn't help but feel a little better about what he saw yesterday. A bit more optimistic, at least. He'd stand by James. He and Aiken would. They'd do what they could for as long as needed. He'd be alright. James always landed on his feet...

"I'm fine, *thanks for asking*. Late night, but you know... I'm still young... well, younger than you at least," he smiled smugly.

Tony scowled. He could give it, but never liked to take it.

But that was the joy in winding him up so frequently.

The summer holidays might have been a bit tedious, but at least they were an easier time to work in the coffee shop. Less early morning footfall, presumably due to parents taking their kids away. It was nice because he didn't think he could handle being rushed off his feet so soon after arriving. The autumn months were the worst, and there was no chance he'd rock up to work during October with the hangover he had this morning. People could shove those Pumpkin frappe-latte wotsits where the sun didn't shine. *Steamy Beanz* didn't even sell them, but customers would come in daily asking for them as though they were a standard British coffee shop order. They weren't and never would be, if Billy had anything to do with it.

He could just about cope today, he hoped, and there was something he did want to talk about without the rush of customers getting in the way.

"I met her," he grinned sheepishly across the empty café

floor.

"I beg your pardon? Oh Billy, you always do this, you loon... I'm not psychic, you know." Tony chuckled, as he should have known what his colleague was like. "Met *who*?"

"Dana," Billy said, as though it was plainly tattooed on his forehead.

"Again, I repeat. Dana *who*?"

"Oh shit. I haven't told you any of this, have I? *D uh.* Dana's my surrogate. You know. We're gonna have a baby, right? I did at least mention that, *once or twice*?"

"Does that mean you're not going to adopt anymore?" he asked, trying to keep up.

"Well... I don't know. This kinda just came out of the blue. I was just making enquiries online; in a couple of forums, and it all just fell into place. This way, we could have a baby in the next year if it all goes to plan. But don't say anything because I've not even told Aiken about it yet."

"He'll love that," Tony said, rolling his eyes.

Tony knew enough about Aiken to know exactly how he'd react when he found out his perpetually optimistic husband had arranged all of this as a surprise for him. From what he remembered, Aiken wouldn't necessarily take it so well, either.

"So, who is she?"

"Dana."

"Anything else? Does she have a surname? A job. A face? Or is this Dana just a floating womb waiting to be impregnated by a few of your finest swimmers?"

"Ugh, gross. Here, look," he offered, pulling his phone out. "I found her on a surrogacy Facebook group. You're not actually allowed to advertise or ask for surrogates, but she contacted me a few weeks ago, saying she liked my profile and wanted to help me."

"Sounds fishy to me."

"Well, she is a lesbian," Billy laughed, even though Tony rarely got the LGBT references.

"I'm really glad, though," Tony went on, ignoring Billy's 'joke'. "I've heard all about the adoption agency. The waiting list is so long now. I didn't like to say anything before, but my friend Sally, you know the social worker, she said you'd be on the waiting list for months, years, probably before you'd even be up for consideration. I'm pleased, so long as it's all above board."

"Yeah, course it is. She knows what she's doing. This'll be the fourth time she's been a surrogate for someone now. I've even messaged one of her other gay dads she's done it for and he said she was amazing. He couldn't stop singing her praises and he even wanted to use her again for his second, when the time was right. I need to get in there first though, before anyone else gets her up the duff!"

"Wow. You've got it all figured out, haven't you? Let's take a look at her then."

Billy eagerly unlocked his phone and opened Facebook. Scrolling back through Dana's profile, there were many pictures of her. Some in which she was holding babies. Billy even pointed out one of her surrogate dads; Johnny, as he was tagged in a few of her photos, too.

"She seems nice. I'm pleased for you... it's so exciting. You must be made up!" Tony grinned, somehow thinking she looked familiar, but for the life of him he didn't know where from.

***

On Thursdays, James and Cleo had a longstanding playdate with Leigh and Mia. With Billy at work, it meant nothing had to be re-arranged, or amended to accommodate a demandingly clumsy and rather hairy thirty-four-year-old houseguest. With the weather predicted to be so nice, they'd arranged to meet up at Millbrook Park, where they'd let the kids run about, play on the slides and get an ice cream.

Once again, the morning was beautiful and James was cursing himself for not bringing a hat to cover his ever so slightly thinning hair on the crown of his head. At least Daniel wasn't around to say 'I told you so', when he'd end up with a red patch this afternoon.

"Hey honey. How's things?" Leigh called over before giving him a big hug. "Hello Cleo."

"Mia Mia Mia!" he shouted excitedly.

Straight away, the two kids trundled off to play in the sandpit. She was trying to hug him; he was trying to break free. Standard toddler stuff, by all accounts. Why was it always the little girls that were more affectionate when all the little boys wanted to do was go and play? James could almost picture the two kids as a frustrated middle-aged couple, at it like that. Cleo wanting to go down the pub, with Mia crying that he never gave her enough attention or bought her enough gifts. He would have laughed if it wasn't a little too close to home for him.

James handed Leigh a paper cup filled with almost-drinkable coffee, and they made themselves comfortable on one of the benches facing into the playground.

They were fortunate enough to have a place like this on their doorsteps. Perfect for the little ones, and with the café there, it wasn't bad for the parents either.

"Not too bad, thanks. How's Mike?" he asked.

"He's great. He was asking after you, actually. Said you all should come over one Sunday for the kids to play in the garden."

James and Leigh had never met each other's partners before. Bumping into each other about six months ago, their friendship had started with a nod and a smile, and developed from there, but was constrained by their non-working free-time during the week, so far, at least.

"That'd be nice. You're so lucky with him. I'm super jealous of how hands on he is with Mia. What I'd give... anyway. Yeah, we'd love that."

"I take it Daniel hasn't been much better recently?"

"What do you think? James grumbled, reactively pulling a face. "I asked him to fix the shower the other day, and he still hasn't come around to do that. He said he'd do it when he moved back. That's just great for me, isn't it? And obviously it doesn't matter how wet the bathroom will get in the meantime because I'll just clean it up, just like I clean everything else up."

"Moved back? have I missed something?" she frowned, a little confused. It had only been a week since she'd seen him.

He proceeded to fill her in with everything that's happened since they met up last Thursday. Because she didn't know any of his other friends, it was easier somehow to tell her everything, including Billy walking in on him naked, Billy falling asleep naked in his bed, the lot. They ended up having a good laugh about it.

"Sounds like he's hot for you."

"Huh. I'm sure you're wrong," he said shaking his head. "I've known him practically my whole life."

"Perfect."

"Not perfect. Anyway, we're both happily married."

She raised an eyebrow at that.

"I am. I know I whinge to you, but I do love Daniel..."

"I know you do," she jumped in, "it just seems that he's never around."

"To be honest, I am getting really fed up of it. I haven't even told Billy this, but I'm just so tired of being his lowest priority. Always. I know I shouldn't complain. He works hard so I can be off with Cleo. We have a nice house, on paper it's all great. But to be honest, I'd rather have him working in Tesco's if it meant we saw more of him, and I had more meaningful time with him."

She laughed. "I've seen your house. No way you'd ever

settle for a Tesco's shelf-stacker for a husband."

"You might have a point," he chuckled.

He appreciated his time with Leigh. She was his friend, and it was nice to have that one person that was his alone. With their secret little conversations that no one else was in on. They hadn't been friends long, but they got one another, and certainly had a similar sense of humour.

"You know what you've gotta do, don't you? Sit down and have a word with him before it gets out of hand. I'm sure it's reparable. Tell him how you feel, tell him what he can do to make you happier, and things will improve. I promise."

"Why is it that you always tell me what I don't want to hear, even if it is exactly what I need to hear?" he sighed. "Come on. I'll get us all an ice cream."

As they got up to leave, he clocked a familiar figure by the booth.

For God's sake, is he stalking me or what?

"Err... on second thoughts... let's just give it another five minutes, shall we?"

"Fine," she said, drawing the word out, "but why?"

"Look at the kids. They are having so much fun."

"And you don't think they'd prefer ice cream? C'mon, cut the crap. What's the real reason?"

"Ugh, just that dick over there. I really can't be arsed with him today. Honestly, it feels like he's following me everywhere I go at the minute."

James really couldn't be bothered to go into it all, but with Leigh's face lighting up at the juicy gossip, he knew he'd have no choice but to tell her everything. She had such a mundane, suburban life, she loved listening to James' tales. Even if they were really old, from way back when. All of her other mum friends were so bloody boring, and only ever interested in talking about their own kid's latest achievements. It was nice to live vicariously through a new friend's colourful youth.

"Spill. And if you miss any detail at all, I'm going to shout him over and insist that he has an ice cream *with* us!"

"Bloody hell, where to start... we used to go out. He dumped me for someone else. We got back together, and he dumped me again for the same guy. I met Daniel and things were going really well. I hadn't heard from Kirk in ages, and then a week before the wedding – on my stag night, he showed up, got me leathered and I kinda ended up at his," James admitted, blushing.

Leigh was sat in shock. Literally, her mouth hung open, her eyes bright and wide. This was a side of James she certainly wasn't expecting. "You slept with him on your stag do?"

"God no. Not quite anyway. I did *go to sleep* with him, but we didn't shag. At least I'm pretty sure we didn't. Anyway. I was off my face, pissed up on drink and God knows what else. Plus, I'm absolutely positive that I'd been spiked that night."

"It was probably him."

"That's what Billy reckoned. Especially as we knew he'd done it before. Anyway, the following day he gave me the whole 'I've changed, I want you back' spiel, but by this point I obviously wasn't interested. I was, *am* in love with Daniel. He threatened all sorts before the wedding, wanting us both to split up so he and I could get back together. Which would have been crazy because I know he'd have ended up getting back with his ex again, anyway."

"So what actually happened?"

"He did. He abruptly left me alone, just like that, and followed his boyfriend to Jersey, where he's been ever since. I don't quite know why, though. Billy would never admit what he did to fix the situation, but that was the last I saw of Kirk until earlier this week when he'd returned again, completely out of the blue."

"He's sounds like quite the troublemaker."

"He certainly is."

"Let's call him over. He sounds like fun," she said seriously before laughing. She took great pleasure in winding him up.

They both burst into fits of laughter, although he was very cautious not to be too loud or attract too much attention. Talking about it definitely helped relieve some of that built up tension and anger.

He never wanted to get into it with Billy again as he'd been so cagey after the stag do. He was sure Billy might have been able to fill some of the blanks but James also had the impression that Billy somehow felt guilty about it, after all, Billy was the best man and completely in charge of the whole evening. James didn't see it that way at all though, and the fear of offending Billy wasn't worth rehashing what had actually happened, especially as it hadn't stopped the wedding from going ahead. The problem was Kirk's and Kirk's alone, especially if he had spiked James' drink.

Sat there, he couldn't take his eyes off his ex now. It was like passing a car accident on the motorway. It was morbid and made him feel sick to stare, but somehow, he just couldn't stop himself. His skin crawled at the thought of what was going on inside his twisted little mind.

Kirk had been so much trouble ever since James had first met him. The best thing he ever did was marry Daniel and put an end to all of that bullshit.

The kids were still happy playing by themselves. They must have been up and down the same slide a hundred times, but they never seemed to tire of it. At least Kirk hadn't recognised Cleo, or spotted James across the park because that was the last thing he wanted today.

Just a few more minutes and he'd be able to get those ice creams.

***

Across town, Duncan was enjoying his lunchbreak in the sun. He didn't always take time out like this, but with Daniel acting a touch awkward around him since they were caught in the act yesterday, it seemed a good idea to give him a bit of space. Daniel could get quite moody when he was stressed, and Duncan didn't want to be at the receiving end of his temper, unless of course he had his legs in the air and was getting ragged about by his boss. So, with the showroom being quiet, it didn't seem a problem to leave Daniel to man the shop for an hour whilst Duncan enjoyed the beautiful weather.

Having just finished his homemade quinoa salad, he took his shirt off and stretched out on the grass in the sunshine. With his hands folded behind his head, he closed his eyes and thought about how quickly the pair had gone from colleagues to something so much more. Daydreaming, he fantasised about how long it would take for them to take their relationship to the next level, and happy he would be when they did. There might have been a couple of hurdles to overcome first, but once they got there, it would be worth it.

The park was filled with kids screaming happily on the play area, dogs barking whilst being walked, and a few others in shirts and trousers, obviously on their lunch too. Above the noise of it all, he heard a voice call out, "You look pleased with yourself."

Squinting in the sun, Duncan opened an eye to see the familiar silhouette of his friend: Tall and lean, he was topped off with a mass of thick wavy hair.

"Hey Sam," Duncan replied warmly, "how's it going?"

Sam took a seat next to him on the grass. "Not bad, thanks. Nice day, eh?"

"Shame I gotta go back to work soon," he replied, not in the least bit disappointed. Maybe he'll get a chance to make it up to Daniel when he returned. Maybe they could even book another night's stay in the hotel this evening.

"So, go on then? What's put that smile on your face?"

Duncan pondered a moment. He didn't know Sam all that well, really. He'd met him through a friend of a friend, and the pair had slowly grown into drinking buddies when out on the gay scene. Not that Duncan went to those bars much anymore. Most of his friends were straight guys into their football and other typically heterosexual interests, so Duncan spent most of his free time with them in working men's pubs and bars in which his friends could pull women. That's where Duncan felt most at ease nowadays.

Other than through himself, there wasn't any kind of link between Sam and Daniel. Their lives never crossed, and they didn't know one another, so it seemed perfectly fine to give at least a little bit away.

But before Duncan had opened his mouth to respond, Sam guessed, "It's a guy, isn't it?"

Duncan's broadening smile did nothing to dismiss Sam's accusation.

"Wow. Duncan in love! Who'd have guessed it." Sam said, nudging his friend playfully.

"I never said I was in love." Duncan replied bashfully, clearly lying. "But I am seeing someone, yeah."

"Go on then... who is he? I bet he's hot," Sam gushed, in need of a bit of vicarious excitement.

"I can't say a lot. It's early days and he's kinda, umm, unavailable."

"Oh my God, you're dating a straight guy, are you? Please

don't tell me you are. It always ends in tears my friend," Sam said, with his tone instantly changing.

"No, but he is..." Duncan began, looking around. Lowering his voice he said, "married."

"No way! You dog." Sam smiled.

The fact was, Duncan could probably take his pick of anyone. Straight, married, you name it, Duncan was stunning and if Sam had ever thought that Duncan would have given him a second look in that regard, he'd have jumped at the chance.

"Well, just be careful. I don't want to see you getting hurt. They rarely leave their wives, or husbands, from what I've heard."

Duncan laid back down on the grass and closed his eyes again. He had ten minutes left before he needed to head back to work, and he hoped that Sam would stick around until then. "What about you? Are you seeing anyone?" he asked keenly.

"Me? What do you recon? That'll be a big fat no. it's so annoying. I don't have any problem getting dates, I just seem to have a problem keeping them. No one wants to date an 'out of work' actor. Honestly, I'd be better off telling them I'm on the dole. Half of the guys out there are now anyway, it seems."

Sam was a good-looking guy and by all accounts a decent actor. "You'll get something soon, won't you?" Duncan said supportively, but to be honest, he didn't have a clue what it was like to work like that, with no security. He'd never seen Sam in anything, either, so didn't know how accurate his reputation was.

"Well, if I don't find something soon, it'll be either shovelling fries in McDonald's or moving back in with my parents."

"Oh God, which is worse?" Duncan cringed.

"I think they're both just as bad as each other. But I will stay optimistic." Sam smiled.

"Well, if you get really stuck, you're always welcome to stay on my couch."

"Thanks man, but I'm really hoping it doesn't come to that."

"Or, maybe you could come work with me and Daniel? Business is doing really well at the moment. He's teaching me so much and if I can start working in the back more, there might be an opening on the shop floor," Duncan suggested, briefly wondering how fun it would be to own and run *Coben Oak* with Daniel.

"Is your boss that fit older guy I saw on one of his *Coben Oak* posters? I might just come and work for him anyway. He's absolutely gorgeous."

"Hands off," Duncan said playfully. "He's taken."

The pair chatted some more, catching up on mutual friends mainly, before Sam walked Duncan back to work. Duncan had the distinct feeling that Sam wanted to catch a glimpse of 'that fit older guy' in action, but didn't let on. He'd save that news for another day.

The Previous Friday

Twelve

Ready to pack in his habit, Aiken had vowed that the next flutter would be the last. It *had* to be. He couldn't keep going on like this. Keeping things from Billy, lying, staying away from Broderick. He couldn't keep it up much longer. His nerves were shot to shreds as it was.

But he was sure this last one would be the right one. He'd followed all the 'hot tips' online and had made a few connections via social networks that all knew what they were talking about. He wouldn't usually bet on the races at Sandown, but with the fact that 'Journey's rush' had such an outside chance (and was secretly tipped to win amongst Aiken's trusted advisors), it seemed the perfect swansong for his habit. It would get the bank and Broderick off his back all in about eight minutes, all things going well. Maybe under, if the horse was as fast as some of the predictions he'd heard.

William Hill's maximum pay out was currently two million, whereas *Ladbrokes* was just one. But with better odds, and therefore lower stakes on his horse, he chose the latter bookmakers instead. Less of a risk financially, but still a huge, 'would certainly get him out of his hole' pay out when he won. He didn't want to be greedy, and it was therefore the better choice.

More confident than he'd ever been in the bookies before, he placed ten grand on the horse to win. With a hundred-to-one odds, his payout would have been one point zero one million, but what the hell... he didn't mind 'losing' ten grand due to *Ladbrookes'* cap.

He'd nipped out of work, paid up and went to sit in the park to watch the race on his phone. With the sun beating down on him, he felt relaxed and at peace; grateful that his betting days and his financial insecurity would be over very soon.

In fact, he might even take some time off and treat Billy to a really nice holiday.

***

Daniel was pacing up and down outside the back of his workshop, trying to clear his head. Even with the main road so close, he'd always felt relaxed here. The woods that backed on to his car park made it feel like he was almost in the country, and the constant hum of the birds and the bees usually put him at peace.

Today, though, there was a sinking feeling in the pit of his stomach that told him something was off. And he knew exactly why that was. He'd barely heard from James in the past couple of days, except to complain about that bloody shower door, which was odd in itself. He'd usually be texting stupid memes, or sending little notes all day long, but this morning he hadn't even *WhatsApped* a daily picture of Cleo. It was so unlike James, and it had Daniel wondering if he'd somehow found out. That fear was always hanging at the back of his mind anyway, but with the lack of communication, it now seemed a real possibility. The reality of what might happen if he was caught was finally sinking in. Should he call and check everything was okay himself? Being so out of character for Daniel, though, he worried that it would probably raise more suspicions than it resolved.

But it was still early and knowing how long Cleo could sleep, he wondered if James was still in bed. Maybe he'd give it another hour and then call. The waiting wouldn't help his nerves, though.

Splashing the dregs of his now-cold coffee onto the ground, he noticed something on the gravel by the door.

"Ahh."

It was that the box that had been delivered on Wednesday.

He thought about that moment and wondered again if it had been James that had caught sight of them. *Surely not?* But then, that could explain James' comms blackout this morning.

He had hastily forgotten about the parcel the other day, more preoccupied with trying to see who it was that what had been dropped and he'd failed spectacularly at that.

Usually confident, he wasn't used to the anxiety of not knowing, which was beginning to churn the contents of his stomach. All because he'd got too cocky and left the door wide open for anyone to see. To think he had enjoyed the danger of it all, that was, before actually being caught in the act.

He was tempted to turn around and go back inside. If he didn't open it, maybe it wasn't real. Maybe he could still pretend they hadn't been seen by someone.

Curiosity soon got the better of him and within moments, Daniel had bent down for a closer look. As though cautious of what it might contain, he examined the package carefully before touching it, or picking it up.

It was about five inches by eight, and maybe three inches tall. Turning it over, he read the writing – addressed to him – on the top of the box and knew who it was from straight away.

Why had this even been posted?

Did he send me this to cause trouble?

Was I caught out on purpose?

As if scared of being seen, he grabbed the parcel and took it into the workshop. He closed the door tightly behind him. Irrespective of the heat, or the cool draft the open door offered. He just needed to block out any prying eyes and focus on this 'gift' and the problems it had created.

Carefully peeling the paper away, he lifted the lid. Inside the box, he found a smaller box of his favourite dark chocolates and a naked, *fully erect* photograph of Duncan, stood right there in the workshop. Daniel remembered the moment well. He'd taken the picture himself.

Across the top of the image, Duncan had written; *'Take me*

whenever you want me'.

His nervousness quickly turned into rage. This had all been avoidable!

Furious, he threw the box to the floor, but not before taking the photograph first. He couldn't let this evidence out of his sight. On hitting the hard floor, the chocolate box bounced out, sending the best truffles he'd ever tasted rolling in every direction. But he didn't care.

He just couldn't believe it.

Daniel genuinely couldn't believe Duncan had sent it at all, much less to his home address when he knew Daniel wasn't even there to receive it.

For fuck's sake. What the hell was he playing at?

"Duncan? Duncan... where the hell are you?" He shouted, storming through the workshop onto the shop floor.

"Hey handsome. What's up?" he asked with a nervous smile.

At least there were no customers at the moment. Not that it would have stopped him, in the rage he was feeling right now.

"Did you want us to get caught?"

Duncan hadn't seen him like this before, and didn't quite know how to deal with it.

"Pardon?" he asked nervously.

"Did you do this on purpose so we would get caught?" Daniel shouted, holding the photograph inches from his face.

"No, of course not. It was meant to be a nice surprise. I

thought you'd like it," Duncan explained, hurt at the accusation or the thought of having to explain his kind gesture.

"You sent a photo of you with your fucking cock out *to my home address*, knowing I'd be at work when it was delivered, and you don't think there's a problem with that?"

"I didn't think..." he said, coming over for a kiss. "I'm sorry."

Daniel was visibly agitated. Red faced and angry, he looked like he was about to explode.

"You need to go. Take the rest of the day off. I can't be around you today like this. I need to calm down. I just can't look at you right now."

"What?" he asked, totally confused.

"Get out. Go. Now, before I do or say something I'll regret."

He didn't quite understand what was going on, or what the big deal was. "Are we still on for next week... the hotel again?"

"Duncan. If I haven't already made it perfectly clear, we're through."

Motionless, Duncan couldn't move. Upset, he just stood staring into Daniel's eyes.

He wanted Daniel so badly. He needed him.

Duncan did want Daniel to break it off with his husband, of course he did. He was head-over-heels in love with his boss, had been since day one, really. But that didn't mean he'd sent the parcel with the sole purpose of being caught by James, though. It was supposed to be a nice surprise, not something that would piss Daniel off so much that he didn't want to see him again.

Daniel was everything. Successful, handsome, well stacked, *well hung...* he was the total package and Duncan didn't want to give any of that up, especially over a stupid mistake over a silly little gift like this.

This could all be sorted out? It would all blow over, surely?

He stood there for a moment, dumbfounded. Not quite understanding what had happened, or why Daniel was so mad at him.

"I love you Daniel..."

"It was a silly affair. Nothing more." Daniel spat, before adding, "and now you need to go. I'm so fucking mad with you right now."

"But what about work? You can't just fire me..."

"I can't even look at you right now. Take the rest of the week off, and we'll see what happens on Monday. Go. Now!"

He hadn't intentionally tried to sabotage their relationship. *Had he?*

Duncan grabbed his stuff from behind the till and left without another word.

He just needs space. He'll come to reason. I know he loves me.

"This isn't the last of us," Duncan promised under a hushed breath. "I just know it isn't."

With his head hung low, he dragged his heels to the front door and was gone.

Daniel stood there, watching Duncan leave. There was no chance he ever wanted Duncan to step foot in *Coben Oak* ever again.

That would be far too risky.

He was so angry with Duncan. If he hadn't sent that parcel to his home, it would never have been dropped off at the workshop. They wouldn't have been caught and none of this would be up in the air. He still didn't know if it had been James or not that had seen them, but either way, the whole jig was up.

Fucking hell.

What had started as a manageable bit of convenient no-strings fun had so quickly evolved into a situation far more complicated than Daniel had bargained for. If he'd have known it would end like this, he'd never have stripped off for his assistant in the first place.

He didn't like that threat, either. He knew that Duncan could be a bit of a loose cannon. After all, it was him that began the affair. It was him that seduced Daniel in the first place, not caring about Daniel's husband, or child at home. It took some balls to hit up your married boss, didn't it?

Daniel had to manage the situation very carefully, and limit the damage as much as possible. Take the lead and make sure none of this shit got worse.

Above all, assuming he didn't already know, Daniel had to prevent James from finding out what had happened yesterday.

Fuuuuuck!

Pacing through his showroom, Daniel tried to calm himself. He needed to think rationally if he and his marriage were going to survive this little mishap.

How could he have been so fucking stupid?

How could he have done it at work, where anyone could have walked in?

Still a little agitated, Daniel decided the best course of action had to be checking in with James. There was no way around it. He had to make sure it hadn't been him that had walked in on them. He certainly wasn't going to come clean just yet, but he could at least gauge if there was really anything up with James like he had been concerned about.

Using his mobile, he apprehensively called his husband, not quite sure if he wanted the conversation or not.

Pickup dammit. The one time I really need to speak to you and you aren't bloody answering...

Ring ring. Ring ring.

"Hey honey. Have you missed me? I hadn't had my usual update this morning, so just wanted to check in with you to see how you are. And Cleo. How's my little fella doing? Give me a call. Love you."

Fuck. Why did I have to end the call like that? Now he's going to know something is up...

***

"You're home early. What's up? Hey, come here. What's wrong?" James asked.

Billy had burst through the front door in tears. James had seen him like this before, but it wasn't common for him to cry. There must have been something seriously wrong.

"Hang on a sec," James said, pulling his phone from his pocket before switching it to voicemail.

"I can't believe it," Billy sniffed, going in for a much-needed hug.

"What's wrong? I'm sure it can't be that bad."

"Dana. That stupid cow was lying from the start... and I was stupid enough to fall for it."

"Lying about what? What's happened?"

Billy pulled away. His face was a mess. He'd been crying, and he'd obviously wiped that and maybe a bit of snot even, across his face. James barely noticed. He pulled him back and squeezed him tighter.

"Tony knew her. Well, he'd seen her come into the café earlier this week. She's been scamming me right from the start. Her and her fucking *husband*. She was all over him and Tony saw it all."

He'd barely stopped for air. Clearly upset. There were tears, blubbering, the works and it pained James to see him so upset.

"Hang on a sec... I thought she was lesbian?"

"So did I, but it was all lies... Apparently, they were never going to go through with it. They are local, and not from 'out of town' like she said. That money I'd transferred for transport and hotels. That was a scam. All of it was a lie. She was raking it in, then going to pretend to get pregnant and then when she 'lost' the baby, she'd try again. All at my expense!" Billy took a breath. He was obviously agitated, worked up and angry, and rightly so. After a sniff, he continued, "Tony did some digging on that website and they'd tried it on with another gay couple about twenty miles away."

"What about that guy that you contacted, the one that said she was a great surrogate?"

"That *was* her husband. That's how Tony put two and two together in the end. He recognised her *and* him from the pictures when they were in the coffee shop."

"Stupid bitch. What, she wasn't even smart enough to avoid where you worked?"

"I guess not."

"Fucking hell. Wow! I don't know what to say, except sorry..."

"Thanks."

"At least you didn't give her much..."

Billy stood there with his head hanging low. He didn't want to even thing about it anymore.

"Err, what else did you give her, Billy?" James pressed.

"What, you mean... *a sample?* No, not yet, thank God, but I guess she was only going to dump it, anyway. I had paid to put her up in a hotel, and for her travel. I'd paid towards her meals out as well."

"Could be worse, I guess..."

"Not by much. The way Aiken has been recently, I reckon this was the last thing keeping us together. You know what he's like with me. No emotion. No affection. He already thinks I'm an idiot at the best of times. When he finds out I've wasted hundreds of pounds on a con artist, he's never going to let me try surrogacy again."

"You still have the adoption, though."

"That's never going to happen though, and after this fuck up, I bet Aiken puts a stop to that too. I'm obviously not fit to be a parent." He began to cry again.

James thought about their relationship. He knew that Aiken was rather cold, and that he rarely showed emotion, but he did believe they were in love, and that Aiken wanted to be with him. Thinking about his own husband, he couldn't in all honesty say the same thing.

James squeezed his best friend one last time, before leading him through to the kitchen.

He poured them both a large glass of wine and they went to sit down and drown their sorrows.

"It's going to be alright; I promise."

***

Aiken hadn't gone back to work as he'd intended. He couldn't stay there, not in his state. He certainly didn't want anyone to see him like that. Nervously shaking, on edge and now fearful of what lay ahead.

He needed to get some air. He'd made his excuses to Silvie, claiming there was a family emergency (there was, he supposed) and that he'd have to close the shop for the rest of the day. She said that Broderick had been back in asking for him again. *Typical.* That was yet another reason not to go back!

Silvie had offered to hang around and keep it open, but he was too nervous to think about it and he didn't want Broderick popping back to ask her questions. That would only make matters worse. She didn't mind some time off in the sun, in the end, particularly as there hadn't been any pre-orders for the afternoon.

Aiken's drive back was horrific.

On one hand, he needed Billy. He'd never 'needed' anyone in his life before, but now, somehow feeling like a small child who had done something so fundamentally wrong, all he wanted was a hug from his husband.

On the other hand, once Billy had found out the extent of his problem, he probably wouldn't stick around long enough to help. He was so sure that Billy would leave him after this, and it scared the life out of him.

By three-fifteen, he was back home with a scotch in his hand. Just as he was taking a first sip to try and calm his nerves, the door burst open and Daniel flew in. He'd almost spilled his drink at the surprise of his entrance.

Red faced and huffing about, it didn't take long for Aiken to realise that Daniel was in as bad a state as he was.

Somehow it helped. *Slightly.*

"Looks like you need one of these," Aiken offered.

"Make it a big one. Fucking hell..."

"Want to talk about it?"

"Definitely not," Daniel said sullenly, before adding out of politeness, "but thanks anyway."

"Mind if we talk about mine? I don't know what I'm going

to do," he said, with his head held low.

"Sure. Anything to take my mind off my little *predicament*," Daniel said, swirling the ice around in his tumbler.

They miserably clinked glasses and went through to the lounge to make themselves as comfortable as their situation allowed.

Aiken had filled Daniel in on the latest details. They all knew he liked a flutter, but hiding his finances as well as he had, no one knew how bad it had got over the last year, or how much money he'd been losing recently.

"I was so sure that the bet on today's race would come through. It would have been enough to pay off all my debts... I was wanting to concentrate on Billy and the impending adoption. Now, it looks like I'll probably have to sell the house, or the business. Ten grand! Ten bloody grand that I really don't have to spend in the first place. I don't know what I'm going to do."

"Fucking hell. I thought I had it bad." Daniel sighed, with his eyes wide and eyebrows raised.

"Neither prospect appeals, and either way, Billy is going to be furious. That's just to start with, I'm sure he's going to dump me. Who wouldn't?"

Daniel went through to fetch the bottle of scotch. They were going to need it this afternoon, that was for sure.

"You'll be fine. Billy loves you. It's like James. I could do pretty much anything, and he'll always be there for me," he said, hoping it to be true.

It took another two *large* rounds before Daniel confessed

to what he'd been up to with Duncan, and how they had been caught by someone as yet unknown.

Under the influence of adrenaline and alcohol, they'd both agreed to keep their little secrets to themselves. Daniel had persuaded Aiken not to tell James (or Billy) at all, and in return, Daniel wouldn't mention anything about Aiken's money issues either. Aiken knew he had to tell his husband about the money, but this could wait until tomorrow... or the next day. After all, there was no sense in making a big deal tonight, already half-cut and upset.

***

It was still early, but as the boys had also had a rough day, the drinks were flowing just as readily.

Like their husbands across town, James and Billy had tried to find comfort at the bottom of a glass.

"How are you holding up?" James asked.

He was sitting on the couch, with Billy cuddled up, half laid on him. They both appreciated the closeness.

"It fucking stinks. I'm angrier at myself than anything else, I think. What a thick bastard I am for doing something so stupid. I should have known it was too good to be true."

"Don't. It was an easy mistake to make. You want to be a dad so bad; I don't blame you for trying. And you didn't waste too much money on her, did you?"

"Just a few hundred."

"Can you shop her in? Call the police?"

"What's the point?" Billy sighed. "I'd rather just forget about it. It's not like Aiken will notice what I've wasted, I don't think, so that's a bonus, I guess. But more than the money, it's the fact that I thought we'd be getting pregnant soon. I thought that we were once step closer. That's what makes it so much worse."

James ran his fingers through Billy's hair as his head lay on his lap. The intimacy was nice. Neither of them had really been able to do stuff like this with their husbands. They just weren't interested, usually getting frustrated, or pulling away. But between the two friends, it was nice. Reassuring, even.

Maybe there was some truth to their jokes on Saturday about him and Billy, and Daniel and Aiken making better couples than they were with each other. But then, opposites were supposed to attract, weren't they, which is probably why they'd ended up as they had.

"Thank you," Billy said, subdued.

He'd finished his third glass and was content being stretched out, with James fussing over him.

"I'd do anything for you."

"I know."

Billy rolled over, nuzzling his face into James' soft midriff. It was nice. Comfortable. Homely, somehow. James thought he might be crying, but didn't want ask, or make Billy more embarrassed than he might already be.

James felt odd. For anyone looking on, the situation should have been overfamiliar, or inappropriate somehow.

But for him, it was perfect. It was for Billy too; he could sense it.

They never usually fussed over each other so much. It must have been this strange week they were sharing, because usually it would be joking around, or even one or two play fights. They were always close, but this was certainly more intimate than what they'd been used to.

The pair sat in silence for a while. Eventually, Billy looked up. He was going to say thanks. He should have said, 'it should be me looking after you, after what your husband has been doing', or 'it should be me protecting you from Kirk, like I'd tried to do years ago'... but he couldn't. He didn't have the heart to break James'. Not tonight, anyway. Instead, he did the most natural thing in the world. He reached up and kissed James fully on the mouth.

James kissed him back as though it was a handshake or a man-hug. It just felt so normal between them. Right, even.

Momentarily, they pulled apart. Not out of shock, or mistake, but to tell each other it was okay. What they were doing felt like the most natural thing in the world.

Billy got up, mindful not to flaunt his budding erection, and took James by the hand. Leading him upstairs into the guest bedroom he'd been staying in, he turned around to face James once more.

"I don't know if this is a good idea, but I want it more than I've ever wanted anything before."

"Me too," James said, pulling Billy in close for another embrace.

Moments later, they slowly began to undress one another. This wasn't in-the-heat-of-the-moment titillation. This actually meant something between them. It wasn't cheap or tacky, and however many hearts they were going to break, they both knew that tonight, at least, it wasn't a mistake.

Taking the lead, James gently lowered Billy onto the bed, following close behind. They couldn't stop touching one another. It wasn't cocks or asses, but their lips that were important.

Rolling around now, both naked, it was obvious that neither one of them wanted it to stop.

James levered himself over his best friend. Kissing, nuzzling, squeezing and cuddling, he couldn't get enough, and he knew it wasn't the wine that was causing their magnetism. This was something far deeper, and far more important. Something that had been inside of him pretty much since the first day they'd known each other.

Sliding his hand down Billy's slightly hairy, stocky side that he'd found amazingly attractive, he took hold of his thigh, pulling it up next to his own. He liked the feel of the rough, curly hairs under his fingertips. By this point, both men were turned on like they hadn't been in years. Thick, stiff and already sticky at the tip, they were both eager to share themselves and be as close as possible.

Billy slid his hands around, pulling James into him by the buttocks.

"Make love to me," he whispered.

He was already so wet, and with Billy relaxed and eager,

James managed to slowly inch his way in. The warmth felt incredible. Both the love-making and their deep connection with one another.

James didn't want it to end. He slowly pulled himself out, almost to the tip, before gently sliding himself back in as deep as Billy would allow.

"Ahhh," he groaned euphorically. Unfamiliar of late with topping, the novelty was as exquisite as his company.

Billy wrapped his arms around his lover. Pulling him close. Needing the physical connection. Body on body, skin on skin. He began to cry. Small quiet tears that James acknowledged with a passionate kiss. He felt the same. Overcome with tingling emotion, far deeper than he'd ever experienced before. This was the real deal. This is what making love was about; actually feeling love and emotion, wanting to please your partner, rather than just yourself.

The couple, now entwined in a mass of legs and arms, again pulled into one another before rolling over. Then Billy was on top, slowly riding James' large, hard shaft.

Bending low, he kissed James on the lips. Then he trailed his tongue down to James' ear, his neck, and then kissed from the underside of his bicep into the pit of his arm.

"Hmmmm," Billy groaned, taking in James' masculine pheromones.

Squeezing his buttocks together in time with his rhythmic motions, Billy took each of James' hands in his own and stretched them out on the bed above his head. Trailing his fingers gently back down them from the wrists, inner forearm, down to James' pectorals, and then stomach, Billy finally wrapped his hand around his own member, slowly sliding the skin back in time with himself making love to James. This was to turn James on just as much as it was for his own pleasure. His grin told Billy that it was working.

Every inch felt amazing. With James inside of him, he'd never felt so full. His own cock, too, felt more sensitive than it ever had before. This was what ecstasy felt like.

Bending low, Billy whispered he was close to cumming.

James drew his hands down to Billy's buttocks. Loving the feel of a little extra flesh down there, he cupped Billy's arse, lifting and lowering it onto his throbbing cock, which too was ready to bust. He could feel the familiar tingles of an impending orgasm. Wanting them to stay at bay as long as possible, yet eager to experience the moment with his best friend.

Leaning up, James wanted to be kissing Billy for this milestone. After twenty years, the first few of which were seriously besotted with this man, they were finally going to climax together for the very first time.

"Ahh," they both groaned in unison.

James spilled himself into the warmth of Billy just as Billy's lower half was contracting in its own thrill of orgasm. The tightness of him, along with the hot semen that was sprayed across his abdomen, was perfection. James had never felt so satisfied or light-headed before.

Neither had Billy.

Still on top, and still with James inside of him, Billy laid down on his lover's chest, feeling the most loved and most wanted he'd ever felt in thirty-four years.

***

After confessing all to Aiken, Daniel felt that at least a little weight had been lifted off his shoulders. He knew, *hoped at least*, that he could trust Aiken... the one that never talked. The one that always sat on the fence. The one that never caused trouble or kicked up a fuss.

It felt good to talk. Also, the scotch had him feeling a little happier and a little more hopeful. It had been a hell of a fun ride, but it was always going to end, he figured. He'd never wanted it to become anything more than fucking, so in a way, it was for the best that he'd got it out of his system now.

The pair had confided in each other with their darkest secrets, and they both appreciated the release, so to speak.

Daniel could see that Aiken was still struggling. He'd never seen Aiken like this before, and he was clearly upset. After what they'd both been through, it seemed it was on Daniel to cheer him up.

Getting off the couch, he came to sit next to Aiken. He poured the remaining drop of spirits into his glass before clinking a rather melancholic toast.

"To us," he proposed.

"To us," Aiken smiled weakly, knowing really that there was nothing to toast.

"You know, we always get the blame for being terrible

husbands, but we work really hard and have our own stresses that they don't necessarily appreciate." Daniel said, patting Aiken on the thigh.

"True."

"We deserve a bit of slack. We're only human."

Daniel put down his crystal tumbler, took hold of Aiken's and did the same. Turning to him, he leaned in and kissed his now rather tipsy host.

"Woah," Aiken chuckled nervously, not quite knowing what was happening.

"It's fine. We've had a drink. Don't worry about it. Just a bit of fun."

Aiken didn't quite know what to do. Before he could respond, Daniel's tongue was down his throat and he was already starting to unbuckle himself.

"I don't know..." he slurred, unsure of himself or what was happening.

"Come on. You want it. Just relax. We can just have some fun tonight and forget it in the morning. I'm so hard for you." Daniel said, pulling out his dick.

Aiken was now trapped under him on the couch. A little bit of him liked the thrill of it. With the alcohol, he felt looser, freer, even. He hadn't felt sexual in a long time, and it would have been easy to give into temptation here, especially as it was quite literally dangling in his face. In his desperate state, it might even do him some good. It would certainly take his mind off his problems for a while.

"I'm sorry Daniel, I can't," he managed. "I'd... I'd like to, but I love Billy and I don't want to jeopardise that any more than I already have."

"Hey, no problem." Daniel said awkwardly. Pulling away, he struggled to hoist his jeans back up. "It's not a good idea. I think the booze just got the better of us for a moment."

He'd slept with several people over the years. One-night stands, quickies in club toilets, and most recently Duncan. Although he hated it, Daniel knew he suffered from an inherent need to be wanted. A need to be admired and validated by good-looking men. By working hard on his physique, in all his years he'd never actually been turned down before until tonight.

Daniel was a little taken aback. He downed the rest of his drink and wondered if Aiken would regret not taking him up on the offer whilst he had the chance.

James' Stag Do

Thirteen

"Come on, we're gonna head on to another bar soon. Drink up, you lightweight!" Billy ordered.

Lightweight, I don't bloody think so, thought James, taking another hearty swig. *I'll show him how much I can really manage.*

They had already been to three bars, a drink in each, and he was just finishing off his fourth.

"Chug chug chug!" they all chanted around him in a circle.

It was nice to be out with everyone like this. Friends, workmates and a select few family members. He was just having the best night, and he didn't want it to end. They were doing the circuit on Manchester's *Canal Street*. Wearing a veil with a learner plate attached (he'd refused to go out in full drag no matter how much they tried to pressure him into it) everyone they passed seemed to be cheering him on as the stag party made their way, bar by bar, to the club. It was great fun and a night he wouldn't forget in a hurry.

Being social, James was sure he'd make time for them all after getting married. Sure, at twenty-five he was still pretty young to settle down, but he knew what he wanted.

He'd been around the block enough times, that was for sure, although he wasn't really supposed to be thinking about that now he was off the market for good.

"Right, if you don't finish that in one last swig, I'm going to... I'm going to... I'm going to line up six Jägerbombs and make you drink the lot," Penny threatened.

He quite fancied the idea, but decided against dragging out his drink. Everyone else wanted to move on. He knocked the dregs of his pint back and they were all on their way to *Via* next door.

Feeling merry, but certainly not drunk, James hadn't bothered to get involved with whatever spat was happening at the front of his crowd. It wasn't anything serious – he could tell from Billy's tone. Instead, he headed for the bar, intending to order a sensible one Jägerbomb for everyone whilst they decided what they'd have to drink.

Before he'd even turned around, he felt a hand on his behind and could feel the tingling sensation of someone whispering something in his ear.

It was Kirk.

It had been a while since James had seen him. He had to admit, Kirk looked good. Then, he always did. But what was he doing in the bar? It was a long way for him to come to be labelled a coincidence.

"Hey handsome," he said, tantalisingly close.

The pair had last slept together six months ago. James wasn't proud of it. It was during a rough patch he'd been having with Daniel, and it was certainly before they were engaged, but still... he felt guilty as hell about sleeping with an ex whist he was technically seeing his soon-to-be husband. But, if he hadn't been on his stag do, and he'd had a few more beers down him, he might even have been tempted for a quick blowjob in the toilets with Kirk now, just for old time's sake. Who doesn't appreciate a quick blozzer in the toilets on a night out?

"Where's Russell?" James asked, remembering the reason why they didn't get back together properly the last time.

"Through. Finished. Totally dumped me when he realised I wasn't over you," Kirk said with a confident smile.

They were now facing each other. He had slipped a hand down James' front and had groped for his dick.

His grin and his hand told James exactly what he was after. Why he was here tonight... and the only reason was to cause trouble.

"He's getting married in a week," Billy warned, jumping in between the two of them in a kind of body-barricade.

"You always hated me," Kirk said, rolling his eyes like a petulant child.

"I don't like how you treat him. You use him, lead him on, and throw him away when you're done. He's got Daniel now."

"I just wanted to celebrate with him. We're friends now, after all."

Billy looked at James, who just kinda shrugged.

"The more the merrier!" James grinned as he started handing out the drinks. He was too happy, having too good a night to pettily ask Kirk to leave.

Anyway, James could cope with Kirk. Flirting aside, he was in love with Daniel and couldn't wait to marry him. He'd made mistakes with Kirk before, but Billy was right about how Kirk had messed him about over the years. None of that mattered now though, as he wasn't in the least bit interested. Well, maybe just a little...

But even drunk, he was sensible enough not to wreck everything he had with the smart, handsome, savvy hunk of a husband that he was due to marry very soon.

***

James was out of it. From what he'd remembered, he'd had a great night, but now was feeling much drunker than he'd expected to. This wasn't his first rodeo, and he'd been used to drinking way more in the past, but now, somehow, he'd felt far worse than he had in a long time. How had he got so drunk?

He'd remembered losing everyone in the club. Not knowing what had happened or where they'd gone, he'd been lucky that Kirk was there. The sensible adult that obviously hadn't drunk as much as he had.

When James couldn't drink anymore, or find the rest of his group, Kirk had offered to take him back to his hotel room, which was within walking distance, even for a pissed-up James. It saved him getting a taxi by himself, to some hotel he couldn't quite remember the name of.

"Thannnksss Kirrrrrrk. Whadda do without youuu?"

He remembered Kirk helping him with his clothes and he remembered going to sleep.

What James didn't remember that night was that he was rather frisky with Kirk once he'd been stripped. He'd insisted that Kirk remove all of his clothes, too. James had insisted that 'For old time's sake' he gave his ex a blowjob.

He'd also insisted that, one last time before getting married, Kirk should fuck him. After all, Kirk was a dirty bastard between the sheets, and James loved it, so Kirk had told him Unfortunately, James really wasn't himself at all. He was in no position to make decision like that after the amount of drinks and God knows what else he'd had.

That was the night before.

The following morning, however, James felt rough and regretful. He remembered that much, at least. The worst hangover of his life. He could have gone back to sleep for the next week, right up to the wedding, if it hadn't been for the lack of paracetamol, or the sense of abandonment from his friends.

He'd had practically hundreds of missed calls and messages from them all, desperately trying to get hold of him.

His phone had been on silent.

He called Billy to let him know he was okay, although suffering from the worst hangover in his life.

"What the fuck happened? We were in the club until closing waiting for you! We had them turn the lights up and everything. You were nowhere to be found!" Billy had shouted angrily, clearly worried about him. At least now, he was happy to have heard from his best friend, relieved that he was safe and well.

Kirk had brought him up breakfast and was being very attentive when he'd returned looking all bright eyed and fresh faced.

With a hand on James' thigh as they sat on the edge of the bed, he'd told him that he'd changed. He'd promised that it had been a mistake with Russell and that it had been James he'd wanted, *needed*, all along. He asked him to leave Daniel, to call off the wedding, and told him that he'd be making a big mistake if he'd gone through with it.

It was no good, though. James had fallen in love with his fiancé, and was looking forward to the wedding. There was no contest between the two of them.

Things may have been different six months ago if Kirk hadn't run off back to Russell. Things may have been different if Kirk hadn't broken it off with James last year, or six months before that. Or the year before that.

James had been left broken-hearted too many times by this handsome man and his extreme indecisiveness and selfishness. Promises of him changing were useless now, regardless of being true or not.

James thanked his ex for taking care of him last night and was on his way to meet up with Billy even before he'd even finished his coffee.

***

What James and Billy had known for sure about Kirk was that he hadn't changed at all. He liked to stir things up, and he liked to get his own way.

It was only twenty-four hours before the Manchester trip, only two days earlier, that Kirk had been in Daniel's bed.

There was no drink to blame, save for Daniel's usual tolerance of a couple of glasses of red. There were no drugs, no woosy-droosy-ness of being spiked. Kirk was in bed with Daniel because he'd been invited.

Daniel liked having sex. He liked it a lot.

Not a sex addict in the strictest psychological sense, but he got it whenever he could get away with it, and a quick fling with a good-looking acquaintance, however awkward the connection, was just fine by him.

The couple had met up a handful of times in the six months leading up to the wedding, with Daniel wanting to get in as much as possible before his nuptials. He'd promised to knock it on its head, with Kirk and anyone else for that matter, once he'd married James, and he hoped to stick to that. After all, James was a good looking, tall, lean man who Daniel was attracted to. With their many personality differences, but their almost levelled playing field looks-wise, they were a great match.

One last go with his ex, and he'd try his best to be monogamous before the joint mortgage and kids came along.

What Daniel didn't realise at the time was that Kirk felt exactly the same way about James as Daniel did. He wanted him for himself. Now that Russell had broken it off with

Kirk, there was no better time to rekindle his romance with James. His best option was to drive a wedge between Daniel and James, and that's exactly what he was doing on his 'coincidental' trip to Manchester's gay district.

It's not like it was hard work. After all, Daniel was fit as fuck and the sex was great, but it was James that he really wanted. James was a good one. Sensitive, loyal and a good fuck, too. He certainly played harder in the bedroom than Daniel did. Most of the time, Daniel seemed to think being good looking was enough, and rarely put the effort in. James was into the same kinky fun that Kirk was. But James also had the stuff underneath first appearances that most other gays their age didn't have, and that's why Kirk was trying his very best to get back with him.

***

That night in Manchester, Kirk thought he'd hit the jackpot. He'd managed to prise James away from his friends and get him back, willingly, to his hotel room. It had gone far better than he'd expected, in fact. Billy hadn't been the trouble he'd thought he might in the end.

The sex had been great, too, all things considered. And Kirk hadn't felt any kind of guilt about it. In the end, he didn't need to coax anything out of James that James didn't want to do. He was conscious, and demanding it all by himself. All he needed was a little help to relax, slipped in his drink, and he was on top form once they were back in the hotel room.

That night in Manchester was perfect. Kirk's plan to win James back would have worked perfectly if it hadn't been for Billy stepping in last minute and threatening him.

That was a surprise. He didn't know Billy even had it in him, but not long after their night together, he'd made it pretty clear...

Fortunately it hadn't taken long for Russell to have a change of heart and take him back, at least.

Saturday

Fourteen

Duncan hadn't known what to do with himself on Saturday morning.

He *was* scheduled to be working.

He was *always* scheduled to be working on Saturdays, and as usual, he should have been working all day with Daniel.

Saturdays were the one day of the week they spent all of their shift on the shop floor together, which made it his favourite day of the week.

How could it all have turned so sour so quickly?

Duncan thought back to Tuesday night at the Cedar Court Inn. It had been amazing. Their first full night together. Duncan had thought that that evening had been a turning point for them and their relationship. As if they were finally becoming a legitimate couple.

Tuesday night had been the first time they had actually gone on a 'date' together in public. A meal together in a restaurant, then some wine back in Daniel's room afterwards. The evening had been so special. They'd made love, not just fucking, for what felt like hours, and it had brought them much closer as a couple. It must have meant *something*.

Daniel wouldn't have asked him to join him if it hadn't.

From there, Duncan had hoped that maybe Daniel would be considering what to do with his husband and his home life. He knew Daniel wouldn't jump straight into separation or divorce. These things were delicate and needed to be navigated very sensitively, but he'd genuinely thought that they were on the right track for it. He just knew Daniel wasn't faking it when they were making love. He felt every emotion that Duncan had, and then some. He had to...

Duncan knew the difference. He had been with many men before. With his youth and striking good looks, enviable physique and overly proportioned cock, he'd never had trouble in finding a man or two to treat him to the finer things. Now at twenty-one, and having spent the last four or five years on the clubbing scene, it had all become very boring. He wanted more.

There had been no question in Duncan's mind that he was in love with Daniel. Daniel was his first and only love. It was the first time he saw a future, and he was the first man he actually wanted to settle down with. Guys his own age were immature and fickle. That's why he did his best to avoid them. Daniel was mature, and had aged perfectly, yet still had enough youth left in him to be considered 'young'. Duncan was even looking forward to getting to know Cleo better. If Daniel was going to have some kind of custody arrangement with him, that was.

Daniel was everything to Duncan.

The way he fucked him in the hotel... that wasn't just sex.

Duncan knew Daniel had meant everything. Likewise, in the workshop on Wednesday, and a hundred times before then, Daniel was in love with Duncan too. He was sure of it. Daniel knew the dangers of shagging at work, especially with the door wide open. Maybe on some level, he wanted them to be caught. It made sense, because then he'd be forced to come out to his husband and put an end to their relationship in order to be open with Duncan.

Duncan couldn't rest at all that Saturday morning. It felt like he'd lost a limb, but he knew it was only temporary. The shock of having someone catch them. It was the frustration of not knowing who had turned up, not the present itself, which, once he calmed down, would appreciate.

Daniel loved seeing Duncan naked and hard like that. He'd demanded it many times before. He went crazy for Duncan's naked body and couldn't keep his hands off most of the time.

Pulling his phone out, he scrolled through some photographs he'd taken of Daniel.

He knew Daniel didn't like his pictures being taken. He definitely didn't allow naked pictures being taken of him, although Duncan wasn't sure why, as he really loved to flaunt everything he had in front of him as often as possible. Even before they'd started fucking, Daniel loved to take his shirt off in the workshop, complaining that it was too itchy or that he was too hot. He was definitely working shirtless out in the yard long before the weather permitted it. That was all for Duncan's benefit. Wasn't it?

Not wanting his pictures taken didn't quite stop Duncan

from sneaking them, though. Over their time working together, even before they'd started their affair, Duncan had begun taking snapshots. He'd by now amassed hundreds of them since he'd started at *Coben Oak*. Many pictures from afar, of Daniel outside in the sun, shirt off and sweaty... others were of him busy building things in the workshop. Duncan also had some of him just walking through the showroom, looking as handsome as ever.

Duncan had become quite the undercover photographer. He'd even started to enjoy the challenge.

He'd felt that he'd hit the jackpot when Daniel had *insisted* on him staying over at the hotel for many reasons, but most of all for being with him whilst he slept. As soon as Daniel had drifted off, Duncan was able to take all the shots he wanted. Naked photographs of him laid out on the bed. Fuck, he looked so cute when he was sleeping.

Duncan had taken some shots of him blowing Daniel's semi-hard cock whilst he slept. Obviously, Duncan had also revelled in taking several photos first thing of Daniel's morning wood, long before he'd even woken up. He'd taken loads on that hotel trip alone. Next time, he'd even considered trying to sneakily set up the camera before they got down to it. That would be hot, and he was sure Daniel would enjoy seeing himself in action afterwards. It would have been a great surprise for him, one he'd most certainly appreciate.

Duncan had more than enough pictures to keep him occupied until Daniel calmed down and saw sense. It was just the shock of it all that had spooked him. Nothing more, Duncan kept reassuring himself.

Just looking at all the pictures of his boyfriend, Duncan was beginning to get aroused. How couldn't he? Daniel was a god. Laying down on his bed, Duncan unbuttoned his flies and pulled his dick out.

Wanting something a little more risqué, Duncan flicked through his phone's photo albums, searching for his 'hidden' content. That was where the really good stuff was kept. Safely stored away in case Daniel ever did get his hands on Duncan's phone.

Searching through this folder, Duncan lovingly admired the extra-special content of his 'candid' shots of Daniel.

First, there were shots of him holding his son, taken from afar. Those were much easier to take than Duncan would have imagined, with the house curtains usually left open, shots through his living room window were a doddle. During another secret visit to Daniel's house, he'd managed to capture some great pictures of him laughing and joking with people whilst they all sat around his dinner table.

From one of his most prized, and well camouflaged vantage points, were his favourite pictures of all; Daniel sleeping naked in his own bed. It was just a shame that his husband was there next to him instead of Duncan.

As he began to masturbate, the only concern Duncan had now was how to get James out of the picture for good.

***

Kirk was getting frustrated. He'd been back a week now, and he was no further forward with his plans. He wasn't going to sit around and wait for things to happen to him. He had to go out and *make* things happen for him.

He'd started very kindly by being polite. He didn't want to charge in all guns blazing, as he knew that would probably backfire. It had last time, and he didn't know how much James had shared with his husband Daniel about that little episode.

But Kirk was older and wiser than before. Still just as good looking, if he did say so himself, but he'd certainly grown up a little. This time, he had to get it just right if it was going to work.

It had been a wet morning. A thunderstorm that had been a welcome change to the heatwave they'd been having had cleared the air. The streets smelled all fresh and alive with possibility as Kirk made his way across town.

The plan was simple enough. Knock on the door. Suggest going out for a coffee – or better still, be invited in, take it from there... that approach had certainly worked before. Why wouldn't it work again, under the right circumstances? *Take it easy, be yourself and he won't be able to refuse*, he told himself.

Kirk hadn't much else to lose after he'd been sent packing from Jersey. Russell, the guy he thought he was going to gain an awful lot of money from, had kicked him out, leaving him completely homeless and broke. They'd been on-again-off-again for the better part of fifteen years. What was he supposed to do now?

Russell was a fair bit older, and a hell of a lot wealthier that Kirk was ever going to manage on his own. After what happened with James during his stag do, Kirk jumped at the chance to leave for the island of Jersey under the promise of marriage and shared wealth. That never quite happened, and since then, the string of minor indiscretions on Kirk's part had finally caught up with him. Said indiscretions, and Russell learning that Kirk had been siphoning off as much money as he could get away with was apparently the final straw in their 'relationship'.

He had no chance of going back to Jersey now. The end of their relationship, all the evidence, the threats of the police being involved... it wasn't worth it, no matter how much he wanted to stay and patch things up with Russell. No matter how much he wanted to be named in that will of his...

Now Kirk was back home, he wasn't that bothered about Russell or his money anyway, if he was completely honest.

No.

Kirk now had his mind set on Mr Coben instead.

This time, there'd be no settling. This time, he'd really enjoy sleeping with his meal ticket.

***

Billy had to get out of the house.

He needed a bit of fresh air after last night. It wasn't that he regretted anything, by any means, but there was just a lot to process. Particularly with his *and* James' husbands both due over for dinner in only a few hours' time. He'd made excuses to go and get some supplies for the evening and left as quickly as he could.

Although he was pleased, if not a little surprised, about how the evening had ended last night, he still had so much to work through. The betrayal from Dana, his stupidity and the loss of money... Daniel's affair, which he was still keeping close to his chest. All these competing problems were driving him crazy.

Although he could now see that some of the signs were there early in the week, building up into something bigger, the kiss and then the love making had really taken him by surprise. He also couldn't quite believe that he'd instigated it. He never had the balls to do it twenty years ago. Why now, all of a sudden?

Thinking back to last night, he was glad that he did though.

Fucking hell, what a mess!

At least the rain had now stopped, and the sun was starting to break through.

Oh fuck...

As if timed perfectly to shit on his already difficult morning, there was Kirk.

Typical.

What trouble was he cooking up? He never came without fire, so Billy knew it wouldn't be long until someone was in tears, as if he didn't already have enough to processes at the moment.

As if fate was toying with Billy and enjoying every minute of it, there seemed to be no way of avoiding that little problem anymore...

"Billy. Billy!" shouted his shrill voice from across the road, "hey Billy, wait up."

Keeping his head low, he continued to walk. Storming through rapidly drying puddles, not caring if the wet tree leaves were brushing into his face, he tried his best to ignore Kirk and keep going.

"Billy. Didn't you hear me calling?" he demanded, having crossed the road and caught up.

"Leave me alone."

"I was only trying–"

"I don't care what you were trying to do. Stay away from me and James."

"I was actually going to see Daniel."

Billy snapped.

It had all got to him. Against his grain, under so much duress, his rage finally boiled over. Maybe it was just the mention of Daniel, who he was so incredibly angry with. Grabbing Kirk by the scruff of his t-shirt, he picked him up and pinned him up against the wall as if he weighed nothing at all.

"Listen to me, you little fuck-wit. I don't want to hear any of your shit. I've paid you off once, and we had a deal..."

Nose to nose with Kirk, who was several inches off the floor by now, Billy's rage was palpable. Without blinking, he continued, "I don't want to see you hanging around any of us again. You got that?"

Kirk was so taken aback. The sheer dread on his face indicated to Billy that he clearly hadn't expected this. Neither had Billy, for that matter. This was so out of character for him. He didn't know what he was going to do next, if pushed, but it was clear that Kirk really didn't want to find out.

"I'm sorry... I'm sorry. I didn't mean to..."

Red in the face, with his teeth still snarling, Billy dropped Kirk. He stumbled as he landed.

"Now fuck off."

Strangely, the sight of Kirk running back in the direction he came really lifted Billy's mood.

Although not one for trusting Kirk, he'd never seen him look so pathetic before. Knowing his deluded sense of pride meant more than anything to him, he really thought at least one of his problems may have been put to bed once and for all.

Before Billy knew where he'd walked to, he realised he was at the edge of town. He'd just wandered, wanting the freedom of being outside, and here he was. Looking up, he saw the sign for *Coben Oak*, just across the road.

It was tempting to go in and fix another one of his problems. The way he felt right now, he could handle anything or anyone today. Daniel may have the dashing smile, six-pack and muscles, but that wouldn't stand a chance against Billy and his genuine love and protectiveness over James.

He stopped and took a deep breath. He had to remain calm

right now. Although he wanted nothing more than to punch that smug bastard right in his beautifully chiselled face, he refrained. That wasn't his battle to have.

Billy decided to do the right thing and let James discuss the issue with his husband the way he deemed fit.

Fifteen

"Did you get everything you needed earlier?" James asked.

"Huh?"

"Did you sort what you needed to?"

"You could say that." Billy grinned, still a little surprised and *impressed* with how mad he'd got with Kirk. He really hoped that would be the end of it. And if not, he'd certainly enjoy threatening him again if needed.

"I can't believe we're actually going through with this, after everything that's... happened." James said, incredulously.

You have no idea, thought Billy.

"We have to, I suppose. At least we'll get to the bottom of everything," Billy said. "You know, clear the air with level heads and have a grown-up conversation, before..." he paused sympathetically *"moving on."*

"I'm not going back to him. He thinks he's doing me a favour by still being interested in me after all these years. But honestly, I don't even know why he married me. Like he was ever actually 'interested' in me in the first place."

"Of course he was," Billy said kindly, going over to James

to wrap an arm around him, not caring that he would get a little damp.

It was now five o'clock, and they had an hour before the other two were due. Cleo was at the safety of his nana Kath's house and everything else was just about ready for dinner. James had just got out of the shower. With the door *still* not fixed, the floor was rather wet, but at least Billy had every chance of *purposely* catching him naked. Although he'd only come in for a cheeky peek, as Billy had been flitting between rooms as he finished off getting dressed.

James picked a piece of thread from Billy's shirt and gave him a peck on the cheek.

"I know one thing that might cheer you up." Billy grinned, pulling James into him by his towel.

"We can't. Not now..." he started to half-heartedly protest.

Billy was actually intending to tell him about threatening Kirk earlier. He was keen to relive the fear on Kirk's face, such a pathetic man that Kirk was. Billy was going to put James' mind at ease, promising that Kirk would no longer be a problem. But then, hadn't Billy made that promise to James once before?

Instead of coming clean, he chose to let James think he was after some action. He didn't want to ruin things by bring Kirk's name up right before their big night.

It didn't take long, however, for James to change tact. "... oh, fuck it."

He smiled as he began to pull at Billy's jeans. It was still all so fresh and new between them, and most importantly, exciting. He didn't know how the night was going to pan out when their husbands arrived, but he was sure that a quick shag with Billy would help calm both of their nerves in the meantime.

After they made love last night, James had fallen asleep in the guest room, right in Billy's arms. They both slept contently, even better than they had earlier in the week, with the beds to themselves. They woke refreshed and much happier than they had been in a long time. There was no awkwardness this morning, either. It was like a new start. Like they'd woken up to a brand new, happier life. No regrets, no excuses. They hadn't made love again, *yet*, but that wasn't to say they hadn't both wanted to.

It was like starting a sexual relationship after a hundred dates. They knew each other better than their own spouses did. And because they'd never had the awkwardness of sleeping together, and they hadn't dated before, they'd spent the last twenty years talking about each other's conquests, preferences and turn-ons, with more than a few horror stories thrown in. They knew everything about one another, and there were few surprises left, other than the obvious 'what do you look like completely naked' and 'how big is your cock'.

It was strange; they had only slept together once, but James already felt that Billy would be able to please him sexually, and know exactly what to do far better than Daniel ever had.

There was just the matter of their husbands to deal with

first, and that was going to be tricky.

There wasn't a question about him missing Daniel. Of course he would. He'd loved him for years, and that, strangely, was still the case. They had built a stable home for Cleo and there was a certain security in the familiarity of what they had. But that wasn't enough anymore. After spending just a few days with Billy under the same roof and now, with them *finally* discovering a physical relationship, it was clear that James had been missing out on something so fundamentally important to his happiness for a such long time now. However much it may pain him to admit it, it seemed his mother had been right all along.

It was like James had been gasping for air, and he'd only just taken his first breath.

The look in Billy's eye. The kindness and his genuine interest in James, along with the sexual desire that made him feel so special... he couldn't remember the last time he'd had that, and after just seven days, he knew he wouldn't be able to give it up.

And the best thing in the world to James: He looked up into Billy's gaze and it was clear that those feelings were completely and unreservedly mutual. The warmth in his stare, the eagerness to be sexual, and the hardness of him proved they both felt exactly the same way. This wasn't just an infatuation with a new and exciting friend, this was falling in love with your closest confidant of over twenty years all over again in a new and special way. After strained marriages with their indifferent spouses, neither one of them could turn something as deep as this down. There was no question of 'what if he doesn't want to leave his husband'. It was apparent from the moment they first kissed.

"I love you," Billy whispered, before tugging at James' towel, "I always have."

He felt guilty saying it. He'd barely known it was true all this time, not in that context anyway, but it was, and he found himself wanting to say it over and over again. Just saying those words to James made him feel happier and safer than he ever had.

Billy pushed him onto the bed and removed his own shirt just as James had finished pulling down his jeans.

"Show me," he grinned, wrapping his legs around his best friend.

Billy wrapped a hand around each of James' buttocks. He gave them a quick squeeze before pulling him to the edge of the bed. Closer to himself.

With a little saliva, Billy slowly circled his finger into James, who had been so turned on and eager to be fucked that there was little resistance. It felt good for both of them, and they'd barely even begun.

Billy was already damp with excitement. Removing his finger, he pressed himself up against James' opening and gently slid himself in.

"Ahh," James groaned playfully, enjoying the fullness he felt inside.

"You like that?" Billy smiled confidently.

Having James so interested in him had boosted his

self-confidence dramatically in such a short space of time. He'd always been a loud joker and happy to be the centre of attention, but when it came to intimacy, unfortunately, Aiken's lack of sex-drive had manifested itself into insecurities for Billy. However many times he'd been assured otherwise, there was always that dark cloud hanging in the background. Was Aiken's lack of intimacy because he hadn't found Billy attractive?

Now, though, it was clear that James liked everything Billy had to offer. His size, his bulk, his look was no longer something to hide, or cover up, but something that James liked to take hold of. Likewise, with his body hair, James clearly loved it, and now Billy was starting to feel the same way too. James couldn't get enough of Billy. And finally, at the ripe old age of thirty-four, Billy was starting to like himself for the very first time.

"I fucking love it. All of it. I love you Billy, now fuck me," he grinned, desperate for Billy to come inside of him for the first time.

With James' legs held in the air, Billy didn't hold back. He pounded into him with everything, only bending down once or twice to kiss James deeply on the mouth. He didn't care about his wobbly bits. He didn't care that he was getting all hot and sweaty – after all, James had told him more than once that he liked a 'good old sweaty shag', if only he'd ever get the chance. Well, now he was going to get the chance whenever the hell he wanted it. Billy was going to make sure of that.

All James wanted to do was to grab hold of his lover

and pull him close. His large biceps, his meaty chest, his fuller behind. James couldn't keep his hands off. Running his palms across Billy's hairy pecs really did it for James. Billy was a *real man*, and James loved all of him because of it, instead of in spite of it.

For the first time ever, Billy wasn't self-conscious. He didn't try to suck his tummy in, or go slow as to not build up a sweat. He felt free and was having the best sex of his life because he knew how much James wanted him. This was fun and exciting, and they were both enjoying it as though they were losing their virginities all over again.

He couldn't take his eyes off James, who looked amazing laid out on the bed like that. He looked as good today as the first time Billy fell in love with him, over twenty years ago. Better, even. More masculine. More manly. He was just so beautiful to Billy, and that smile, the smile he wore because of Billy, was worth a million pounds.

Neither of them could take their eyes off one another. Billy lent in for another kiss. His frame bearing down on James felt incredible. All hot and bothered, it was exactly what James craved when fooling around. A real man, really taking it out on his ass. James took the opportunity to wrap his arms around Billy, not letting him go. In tiny kisses, he ran his lips down Billy's neck, onto his shoulder, then down his large bicep.

Knowing what James liked the most, Billy stretched up with his arms to grab hold of the headboard, continuing to work his cock into James as he did.

James couldn't help himself. It was right there, the holy grail of gay sex with a *real man*. Working his lips around Billy's bicep he kissed his armpit.

"Fuck, that's amazing," he groaned, breathing in Billy's fresh, manly scent. His arm was huge. Kissing it again, he ran his hands down Billy's back and firmly grabbed hold of his backside again. Squeezing, he pulled Billy into him as far as he could.

He was hitting all the right spots, and it felt amazing.

"I'm gonna come," Billy murmured with a quiver.

"Come in me. I wanna feel it, and I want to come with you," James begged, barely needing to touch his own hard cock.

Billy had about thirty seconds left in him, if he was lucky. Grabbing both of James' hands from his ass, he slid them up and pinned them on the bed above his head, holding them in place with one large hand. He then took control of James' cock in the other hand. He was already wet and sticky, so it wouldn't take long.

With a final thrust, he exploded into James. His orgasm felt like fireworks and left a tingling sensation coursing through his body long after he was done.

Feeling the throb of Billy's enlarged cock as he came inside of him, James too spilled out from Billy's hand, all over his sweaty abdomen.

He crashed down onto James and kissed him once more for good measure.

I love you, they both thought simultaneously.

"Come on, we'd better go shower again," Billy said, rolling off and out of him.

"Only if we can do it together." James grinned, completely spent, yet eager for more.

Sixteen

He stood pacing across his living room. It was a small room, so it didn't take long for him to make a lap around his *Ikea* coffee table. It was too hot, even though the curtains had been drawn all day.

He couldn't sit for being agitated. This was his future, and he knew it was worth fighting for. He had to do something, at least.

Those words; the warning that was barked at him was frightening at first. Unexpected, they'd come as a shock he wasn't ready for.

But he knew that with a bit of time and a bit of perspective, things would calm down. Things would be better and he'd get what he wanted.

He had to give it at least one last shot. One big gesture to show how serious he was.

He would have to go to the house. He'd go and tell Daniel exactly how he felt at the house.

***

"There's the doorbell. Look at me, you're okay. We can do this, I promise," Billy said, not quite believing it himself. "At least one way or another, it'll all be over soon."

They'd showered again, making sure to wash away any evidence of their extra-marital affair. The scalding water hadn't done anything to cleanse them of their guilt, though. Not so much for Daniel, who James knew would be out on the pull the instant he found out, if he wasn't already, but for Aiken, the unfortunate bystander in the week's messy conclusion.

James squeezed Billy's hand one last time, releasing it just before their husbands entered the living room.

Right away, there was an awkward sense of everyone holding something back. The evening was close, and the clamminess that hung in the air did nothing to help dampen the impending situation.

Who knew what, and who didn't?

It was probable, thought Billy, that Daniel hadn't told Aiken about his dalliance with Duncan, and then subsequently being caught. Billy had barely been in contact with Aiken this week and definitely hadn't mentioned it. So, like James, presumably Aiken was none the wiser, thought Billy.

He was sure too that so far, neither Daniel nor Aiken would know what James and he had been up to, unless of course Daniel had installed hidden cameras throughout the house, which seemed very doubtful.

As was custom for a Saturday night dinner, the four men started with drinks and a game; tonight, Daniel had brought a bottle of Dom Perignon and for no other reason than he was good at it, had suggested they play poker up until dinner was ready.

James was waiting for the obligatory *"You've got to know when to hold 'em and when to fold 'em"* comment – in a terrible Texas drawl, from Daniel. He'd say it every time he won a round, which he'd already done several times by now. This evening, however, for the first time since he'd known his husband, the words just didn't come. James couldn't help notice the poignancy, yet be grateful for their absence. He wasn't in the mood for any of Daniel's wisecracks tonight.

As the cards were dealt and the drinks flowed, Billy noticed that for the first time, Aiken was keeping up with the rest of them, round for round. It was so unlike him.

Maybe he did know.

Both he and James were on their guard, desperate to not let anything slip out until the right time. Their issues were delicate ones, and would be best addressed in the privacy of individual couples. That should definitely be after Billy and Aiken had left for the evening. Or better still, tomorrow.

***

Daniel was nervous, and he was quite right to feel as such. He trusted Aiken enough to believe he wouldn't gossip about the news, but that didn't mean that James hadn't already found out. If only he knew exactly who had delivered that bloody parcel, things would be much easier. He'd hoped it may have just been a delivery man, but that would have made things too simple.

Throughout their game, Daniel had clocked that his husband had been a little cold with him, standoffish, even. Usually, James would have been all over him one way or another. An arm around his shoulder, a hand on his thigh, or maybe just a foot running up and down the back of his calf. After not seeing each other for so long, it should have been a given, but this wasn't the case tonight. Thinking back, had he even kissed Daniel when they arrived? He didn't think so.

Something was definitely up tonight, and it didn't help with his nerves.

On the other hand, Aiken was grateful for the space his husband was giving him this evening. He still didn't know how to broach the subject. It might have been easier for Billy to have found out by his own means. At least it would have saved Aiken a job in coming clean. It was like coming out all over again. He had this news that needed to be discussed. He just didn't want to admit it himself.

Right from the start, he knew he wouldn't enjoy the evening, and just wanted to be swallowed up before anything more was said. Maybe he should just blurt it out, like ripping off a plaster quickly...

The game hadn't lasted as long as it could have. It was clear none of them were 'feeling it.' Instead, they moved through to the dining room as though sitting at the table would make dinner be cooked and served quicker.

***

"Are you going to tell me what's wrong?" Daniel asked firmly, as he stood up from the table.

It was clear that he was getting frustrated. His lowered brow, his huffing and puffing, even at James' more innocent comments. Daniel was working himself up, and it was rubbing off on everyone else.

So far, the booze hadn't helped the ambiance of the evening at all.

Mains had just been served, but it seemed that nobody had the appetite to eat a lot. They weren't much in the mood to talk anyway, and Daniel's strop did nothing to help. Barely a word had been spoken since sitting down to eat and it was clear to all that something was seriously off balance between the four of them.

"What's wrong with me? You really want to know what's wrong with me?" James spat back.

Although out of the blue, once the question had been raised, it didn't take long for the temperature to rise further, and the voices to flair. The two spouses now stood over the middle of the table, inches away from each other's face.

Aiken leaned back in his chair, as though it gave them space. He didn't know what was going on, but he'd never seen the pair argue like this before. Not this viciously, at least.

"Yes. You're acting all weird. Just tell me what's wrong," he repeated, chancing his luck.

James hadn't yet confronted him. Neither had Billy, for that matter. Maybe it hadn't been either of them that had seen him on Wednesday. Maybe that was someone else altogether. Maybe even the postman? "I love you," he added, as if it would make everything alright and his problems go away.

"What is wrong with you? Why are you acting all odd tonight... nice, even? You never show this much attention, and I want to know what's got into you? What are you hiding?" James demanded.

For a night in which he had intended to tread lightly, James had already drunk a little too much. Tongues were flying, and it was going to be difficult to keep it all in for much longer.

Billy couldn't take his eyes off Daniel. He knew the truth. He knew exactly what Daniel had to hide and he couldn't believe he was doing such a good job of it. Had he no compassion or guilt at all?

Billy had felt awful. He should have pre-warned James. He wanted to. He wanted to tell him on Wednesday. And again on Thursday, but he didn't.

He desperately wanted to tell him before they made love for the first-time last night, but he was also conscious, even in the moment, that he didn't want to become a rebound. He didn't want James to ruin their friendship out of spite over Daniel. He wanted James to want him, *regardless* of his husband's cheating. He just hoped now that that wouldn't backfire if James found out that it had been kept from him, which, in all honesty, one way or another, he probably would.

"You don't love me. You've not loved me for a long time," James shouted, finding his inner strength. With so much pent-up anger, it wasn't hard.

"Yes, I do. It's not my fault you let yourself go like this. I've asked you so many times to sort yourself out. I've asked you to lose a little bit, join a gym... go for a run..."

James glanced across at Billy. Looking over, he knew that Billy would never, ever talk to him like that. He was attracted to him for him, not for how thin, fat, tall or short he was. That was real love. He looked down at Aiken sat next to him, who still hadn't said anything on the matter, and could barely hold it in any longer. The guilt was too much.

"What's got into you? I said I still wanted to be with you. That I still love you, even though–"

"What in the hell is wrong with you?" Billy stood, squaring up to Daniel, now furious himself. Why do you have to constantly belittle him? Or me, for that matter. What is your fucking problem?"

"What's it got to do with you? Stay out of it. It's between me and my husband," Daniel poked him in the chest.

Billy shot a glance at James, who was now in tears and had just sat back down.

Daniel caught that look and was by no means foolish enough to miss that it meant something between them. *More than just friends?*

"Calm down Billy. Just let them sort it." Aiken finally piped up, trying to placate the table.

Knock knock knock.

"Who the fuck is that?" Daniel bellowed, now close to tipping point.

This wasn't the time to be interrupted by nosey neighbours or Jehovah's witnesses.

"I'll get it," James mumbled.

Grateful for the distraction, he wiped his face and went to answer the door.

Ten seconds later, Duncan barged into the dining room, with a visibly confused James following close behind.

With a determined look on his face, it was clear he was there to cause trouble. James, on the other hand hadn't a clue what Daniel's colleague was doing at the house, tonight of all nights, but could tell he wasn't happy about something.

"What the fuck are you doing here? Get out! I told you I didn't want to see you again."

"Err, what's going on Daniel?" James asked, bewildered at such a random outburst.

He'd never seen Daniel talk to anyone like that before – well, apart from Billy just now, but especially not his apprentice.

After Daniel had confessed to Aiken, James was now the only one in the room out of the loop regarding the not-so-secret extra-marital affair. Not wanting to be drawn in, or accused of holding back information, Billy and Aiken kept their heads low. Daniel stood at the other side of the table, practically purple in rage. He was going to have to deal with this one on his own.

"Get out!" Daniel repeated, throwing a finger to the door.

But Duncan just stood there, staring at his boss. Not quite sure of what to say. He clearly hadn't planned his entrance well.

"Don't you go anywhere, Duncan. I want to know what the fuck is going on first," James said, his eyes darting between his husband and the apprentice.

Ignoring James, he began, "... but I love you. And I know you'll want me back."

The room fell silent for a moment. In shock. What was there to say to this random outburst?

Duncan advanced on Daniel as if they were the only two people in the room. At this point, he didn't feel the need to try and avoid James' stare. Duncan had no sense of shame or guilt about any of this. As far as he was concerned, it was Daniel leading him on. Daniel was the one that had started this. Daniel was the one that had wanted to leave his husband for him. Daniel was the one trapped in an unhappy marriage to someone that didn't even take care of themselves. James wouldn't be around for much longer, anyway, so the how's and when's didn't really matter. All that mattered was Daniel and Duncan being together.

James was shocked. Stood there, very slowly his mouth dropped as everything started to fall into place.

"Fuck off Duncan. I love my husband. I don't know what you're talking about," Daniel bluffed, a little calmer. Smug, even.

"Huh?"

"I said. Fuck. Off. I don't know what you're doing here," Daniel replied in an Oscar-worthy performance.

Duncan was starting to become agitated now. Nervously his eyes darted about, looking between his lover, the husband and the other two. Clearly, it wasn't how he expected his 'romantic gesture' to pan out, but he was determined to fight for his man, and his job regardless.

"You don't mean that. You love me!" he stuttered.

Daniel laughed. A mean, spiteful laugh. "I don't love you at all. I only *pay* you. I haven't a clue what you're going on about, you silly little boy. I'm happily married with a child. Grow the fuck up and go home."

Duncan lurched forward. Instinctively, James and Daniel jumped back, not knowing what was happening, or what Duncan might try.

"What the fuck are you doing?" Daniel bellowed, now a little concerned himself. Even he didn't think Duncan would become violent.

Duncan reached down and yanked something from his pocket.

"I have these... our photos. Us, together," he blubbered, whilst fiddling with his phone.

"You what? You've been taking pictures of me like some kind of deranged stalker?" Daniel asked, confused and disgusted.

"I love you. We love each other. These are *our* pictures..."

"You're embarrassing yourself in front of my friends and family, Duncan. Just go."

Had he seriously thought that Daniel would drop everything to run off with a twenty-one-year-old twink?

James took a deep breath before calmly saying, "Stay for all I care, Duncan. Daniel, it's over, and that was even before I knew you'd been knocking him off on the side."

"I haven't. I swear!" he lied straight to his husband's face.

Billy would have stifled a laugh at the audacity of it, if it wasn't all so tragic.

It was no good. Daniel could see in James' eye that the secret was out. Clutching at straws, he tried a different tack, "But... but you need me. I don't want Duncan. I want you. I love you."

"No, I don't need you. I need someone that loves me and respects me and wants to be with me. Someone who doesn't make me feel shit about myself. I need someone that is happy and proud and grateful that I'm here. Not someone that would rather I wasn't there."

"If you just lost a couple of—"

"What, to look more like him?" James spat, throwing his head in Duncan's direction. "Do you want me to have a bigger cock too?" he added sarcastically.

"No, Daniel. He doesn't need to lose anything. He's perfect– he's *perfectly* fine the way he is," Billy quipped.

It was apparent that things could get physical at any moment. There was still a terrible tension in the room and although the volume had come down just slightly, there was still a lot of anger, frustration and betrayal in the air.

Duncan was still hanging around, too. Maybe he thought

that now James had cast Daniel aside, there might be room for him. His nervousness earlier had seemed to dissipate slightly.

"Hang on a second..." Daniel quizzed, slowly listening to the dynamic. Reading between the lines. Cottoning on. There was a cruel smirk on his face that radiated jealousy and spite.

"What?" Aiken asked, his eyes darting around the room to each of them. Although he was expecting his own issues to be the cause of all arguments this evening, this wasn't a particularly welcome diversion.

"Don't you get it... Can't you see what's happening?"

"I don't know what you mean," Aiken asked, getting worried.

Was Daniel going to tell everyone about his problem just to take the heat off himself?

Billy sat back down. Wanting the earth to swallow him up, he let his head hang in shame. He was crying now, overcome with emotion. He didn't want it to come out like this. He didn't want to hurt his husband any more than he already had to. He didn't want to embarrass him in front of everyone, either.

"This all makes sense now," Daniel said, more so to himself than Aiken.

"What does?"

At this, James got up and stormed off into the kitchen. With a revelation he couldn't or didn't want to deny, and Duncan still hanging around like a vulture waiting to pick at the bones of his marriage, he needed some space to cool down.

"James and Billy... my husband and your husband... have been *fucking*," Daniel shouted to the back of his spouse.

Aiken sat there in shock. It was hard to take it all in. Unfortunately, he didn't think he needed to ask if it was true or not. It explained a lot this evening.

He loved Billy. He always had, but with his impending financial problems and his gambling addiction, he just didn't have that drive in him to fight for it any longer. If Daniel had been right, it seemed it was too late for that, anyway.

After waiting so long, it seemed that the adoption probably wouldn't happen now. He'd lost a great deal of their money – which he still hadn't owned up to. Why would Billy want to stay with him even if he hadn't slept with James?

Seventeen

The tension in the house had calmed *slightly* after Duncan had finally been thrown out. It would have been difficult for it to become any more awkward, that was for sure.

It took more effort than it should have done on Daniel's part, but he did eventually manage to make Duncan leave. There were some choice words, threats, and a fair bit of shouting, but he finally took the hint and left with his tail between his legs.

What a twat he'd been for coming around like that, causing even more trouble than was necessary for an already stressed evening, Daniel thought frustratedly.

The Fleetwood Mac album had long since ran its course and without the usual drunken chatter, only the sound of the large grandfather clock in the hall could be heard reverberating throughout the house.

Tick.

Tick.

Tick.

It didn't look as though dessert was going to be enjoyed, but it also didn't look as though someone was necessarily going to get punched, either.

That was something, at least.

James couldn't believe it. Or, more accurately, he couldn't believe he couldn't believe it: *Fucking Daniel... shagging his apprentice like that. It all made sense now!*

Why hadn't he seen it coming?

Although James could barely complain himself, after this week's indiscretions, he was still pissed off. Devastated, even.

All the signs had been there for such a long time now. The long hours in the workshop. The lack of interest in sex together. The snide comments and quips about his weight. Was this all about James putting on a few pounds, or was it something deeper? Was he actually in love with Duncan?

Fuck it. It just didn't matter anymore.

"Is it really true?" Daniel asked, more subdued than he'd ever been before. Maybe he'd finally got it. He might actually realise that his last chance of clinging on to his husband was the softer, gentle approach, something he should have adopted years ago, if only every now and again.

He had gone to speak to James in the living room, whilst Aiken and Billy were talking through their own problems in the dining room.

"Yes, it's true," James admitted shamefully.

"I forgive you," Daniel said, saintlike.

"I don't want your forgiveness. And I won't be forgiving you. You've fucked everything up. You've been pushing me away for years and I have finally had enough. Go get your apprentice. You're a good couple. Both of you like going to the gym, obviously. I bet he likes to show off as much as you. You're a perfect match and I think you'll be great together."

"I told you I'm not interested. You just need some time. I know you don't mean any of that, really. You love me, and I know you're still attracted to me. I've ended it with Duncan. It was a silly infatuation on his part. He was chasing me. I wasn't really into it, I promise. It was only a couple of months but its finished. All done. I'll come back home and I promise we'll have sex more often. I'll spoil you. I can buy you more nice things, you know, treat you to stuff."

"You just don't get it, do you? You never have. It's over. Regardless of whatever happens between Billy and me, you and I are through."

Daniel sighed. He just couldn't quite believe it. The last two months had been a silly mistake with a young, attractive co-worker. Duncan was right there and available for the taking. Who in their right mind would be able to resist a bit of fun when it was offered up so readily on a plate like Duncan had.

Daniel had always thought James would take him back. He never banked on him finding out, but then they had been lax, there were so many times that they had pushed their luck at work, it was bound to happen at some point. That was part of the thrill. But Daniel always thought he'd be forgiven and they could just move on closer than what they had been before.

"James, I shouldn't have to beg you, but you're making a

big mistake. If you make me go now, I won't be coming back and you'll regret it. I promise."

The sorrow on his face had been replaced by smugness. James was waiting for him to say something narcissistic. He usually did. 'Look at me, you won't do better than me' 'look how handsome I am'... he'd basically said James was lucky to even be with him in the first place. But Daniel wasn't attractive at all. Not in any of the places that James cared about, at least.

He was sick to his back teeth of it, and just wanted Daniel out of the house.

In the dining room, Aiken hadn't moved. Statue like, his face showed no emotion as he sat staring at Billy. Unable to move. Unable to say anything.

"I'm sorry. I didn't mean it to happen."

What could he do? What could Aiken say or do that would make any difference now? There was a shine that danced on the edge of his eyelid yet refused to actually break into a tear. Showing little emotion, Aiken finally asked the question he was afraid to be answered. "Do you love him?"

"I've always loved him. You know that. We are best friends. We do everything together. But I love you too..." he said, reaching across the table, daring to place his hand on Aiken's arm.

Aiken said nothing. There was no reaction, no flinch, and he didn't pull away. Nothing.

Not wanting to get confrontational, but also needing to use the chance to get everything off his chest, he went on.

"It's so difficult to get anything from you. Emotion, affection, love, or intimacy. I feel like you don't even like me most of the time. It's like a constant state of you just putting up with me and its heart-breaking. I'm really struggling with trying to become a father, and I feel I can't even talk to you about it... even now, right here in the middle of it, it's like you don't care. You've barely reacted to hearing your husband has slept with someone else."

Still staring, Aiken was listening to his husband, but he was finding it hard to *hear* him. Aiken felt as if his head was underwater, and that Billy's words were being washed away under an ocean of debt, stress and uncertainty. He desperately wanted to be a part of everything going on around him, but as usual, he just felt like the outsider unable to keep up.

To Billy, it just felt like he was talking to himself.

"I just don't feel loved and supported by you and it feels like I'm slowly dying."

Aiken took a deep breath. The tear finally broke free from his eye and he said with the most passion he'd ever had, "I love you more than ever, but I've got something to confess myself..."

***

As though nothing had happened, as if their lives were exactly as they had been the previous Saturday, James brought out a large cheese board, a crusty loaf, some knives and plates... the works. It was almost as though everything was back to normal. Just another evening with friends around for dinner.

The clock had not long chimed nine, and if they didn't line their stomachs with more than just a taste of dinner, then the alcohol (of which all four of them refused to stop drinking) would no doubt make matters worse.

Cheese seemed like the only thing they could do whilst stuck in the house with each other; the four friends who couldn't seem to leave until all of their affairs were somehow in order.

Dinner had barely been touched, but cheese felt a better option. *More appropriate.*

After a breather in the garden to clear his head, James felt it only right that the four of them sit back around the table to discuss and decide their next steps, not least of all for the little baby caught up in all of this...

"I just don't accept it. You're making a huge mistake... I mean, look at what you're throwing away." Daniel said, quite literally referring to himself.

James would have loved to have answered him. To have really laid into him, telling him how conceited he was. How his arrogance and ego were so off-putting it's surprising they had lasted as long as they had. James wanted to tell Daniel that regardless of his six-pack, or thick head of hair, or chiselled face, that in fact, he genuinely found Billy more attractive. That Billy was a better lover, knew what he was doing more. *And that he had a bigger dick...* he would have loved to have said that and much more, because Daniel really deserved it. But Aiken; he didn't deserve to hear any of it. He was just caught up in the cross-hairs of a really bad situation.

Aiken was a good guy that had made a couple of terrible mistakes. Those mistakes which may very well have led him to slowly pull away from Billy in the recent years. It was a shame because deep down, he was such a decent man. Maybe not the best lover, but a solid, considerate husband, by all accounts. One that would have made a great father, too, given the chance.

Sat around the table together, James felt more guilt about what he had done to Aiken than he had his own husband.

All of that was too late, though. Billy and James had accidentally yet finally found one another, and both of them knew there was no going back. It seemed that James' mother really had been right all along.

"I love you, Billy," Aiken slurred slightly.

There was a sense of complete and total defeat in his words. He may as well have been waving a white flag.

It had been coming for a long time. Only now could James see it in his eyes. Like his spirit had died, and only now was Aiken finally accepting it himself. The alcohol, of which he'd never really got used to, was getting the better of him. He was finally becoming one of them, it seemed.

Billy couldn't take it. He ran from the room. The pressure of ruining two families was too much to handle. He darted for the toilet, needing a few more minutes before the inevitable *'I'm sorry', 'it's too late', 'it's not you, it's me'* speech.

Billy just needed a great big chasm to open up and swallow

him whole. They shouldn't be doing this as a foursome. It didn't seem right, now. *Oh Aiken*, how could he have let it all get this far?

Fuck the money. Billy didn't care about the money at all, or the house. If Aiken had come clean years, or even months ago, all of this could have been avoided. He only ever wanted a partner, a confidant, a lover. But instead, Aiken had pulled himself away for so long it was now impossible to get back to where they had been, regardless of James and the consequences of their sexual awakening. None of that would ever have begun if Aiken had been a little more present in their marriage.

One more minute and Billy would go back and face the music. He'd tell the truth. They'd work it out. They'd separate amicably. All four of them would deal with the divorces and move forward. For Cleo's sake, it was obvious that they'd have to somehow work out a way to be civil with Daniel. But that boy was the greatest thing to happen to James, and now, Billy too in whatever would come next.

Billy took a deep breath. They had obviously stopped talking since he'd left the room. All he could hear again was the ticking of the clock. Staring in the downstairs loo's mirror, he wiped a tear from his eye, straightened his shirt and went back out to face the music.

Entering the living room, he first noticed James and Daniel, who had on cue re-instigated their argument. Nothing vicious, it was more tit-for-tat about who had actually caused the breakup in the first place. It was all so futile, he thought. Apparently, they'd wanted to spare the expense of blaming one another in front of a delicate Aiken whilst he was a third-wheel. But now Billy was back they had no problem with the bickering, it seemed.

Drawn by James and Daniel, Billy had barely noticed Aiken, or the look on his face. A hollow emptiness that he was at least partially accountable for. It was the silvery blade of the knife that had caught his eye as it momentarily reflected the brilliant glare of the overhanging light into his gaze.

In a swift motion, without any expression, Aiken held the knife, which he had pointing inwards, towards himself. The others, so wrapped up in themselves, hadn't noticed at all. Or cared, maybe?

With a final look towards his husband, Aiken mouthed the words "sorry" before Billy even knew what was happening.

Quickly, he jumped towards Aiken and the blade.

He loved Aiken. He still needed him in his life. They were and would always be family. Forever.

"Nooo!" Billy cried out, trying to wrestle the knife from his husband's hand.

Before he knew what had happened, or how bad it was, Aiken quietly sat back in the chair. With a glazed over look his eye, he finally looked at peace.

Eighteen

There was an abrupt silence that fell across the room. In total shock, James and Daniel were unable to move. Neither of them knew what to do. How to help, or who to go to first. It had all happened so fast. It had really been over before they'd even realised it had started.

So caught up with the drama inside the dining room, they hadn't heard Shirley from next door first of all banging on the front step, they hadn't seen her peering through the open curtains and they hadn't heard her when she'd started to scream.

James' eyes darted left to right. He saw the blood. It was impossible not to see it. There was a lot. Both Aiken and Billy were covered in it from their brief but dangerous tussle.

It was only when Billy coughed, and blood began to spit from his mouth, that James knew it was him who had been stabbed and not Aiken.

Some Time Later

Aiken

It had been a long uphill struggle for Aiken, and one which he knew would never truly be over. The journey had been much harder than he'd ever imagined it would be, but it was one he needed to take. If only he'd started it long before the week from hell...

After the tragic incident with Billy, coupled with his spiralling debts, he felt the only option would be to sell off his profitable businesses. How fortunate it had been for him that Broderick was eagerly ready and waiting to make a deal. Aiken had already lost his flagship location, and it would only be a matter of time before word got out about his finances, anyway. With regards to the rest of his business, what was the point in owning a successful venture when you were unable to manage it correctly, or enjoy the life that hard work and determination were supposed to provide you? At least Broderick was there, ready to negotiate on the initial offer he'd originally left Aiken. It strangely went some way in repairing their long-lost friendship, too. Who knew, maybe they'd end up working together in the future, as well.

With the money that wasn't owed out to banks, bookies, or

worse, Aiken was finally able to deal with his addiction. He checked into a private rehab facility and partook in as many therapies, treatments and discussions as physically possible. He found *Sunshine Lodge* pleasant enough, tranquil even, and was grateful for the time there that allowed him to reassess his life choices.

With the loss of his husband, Aiken was able to focus entirely on his own recovery. Without Billy, or a child to raise, the distractions and temptations of the outside world were easily forgotten.

Learning more about himself than he'd realised, he'd had the opportunity to turn the spotlight on his own demons for the first time in his life. In doing so, he'd been able to commit fully to focusing on his intimacy issues, which had probably been the root cause in preventing him from speaking out and asking for help way back when it might have made a difference.

Aiken soon realised that there was no point in wasting time over what could have been, or what he should have done. There was no point in any of that now. But, with the support provided from *Sunshine Lodge*, Aiken had very sensibly learned to look to the future, rather than dwell on a painful past.

It was an enormous journey from that fateful Saturday night until his 'recovery' (every day is one step further away from his problems), but he was at least grateful of Broderick's offer and the ability to act swiftly, with enough money to fund his rehabilitation.

Aiken was genuinely sorry for everything that he had caused, and he took full responsibility for it, but would never truly forgive himself. He was a different man now, a better one. A little wiser, and a little more rounded, he hoped. It was just a shame he couldn't have learnt all of this before wrecking his career, his life, and his marriage.

Daniel

Amongst all the issues of their final meal, Daniel also had to deal with the aftermath of 'getting his honey from where he makes his money'.

That was a huge mistake, and one Daniel wouldn't repeat in a hurry, no matter how handsome an employee may be, or how much they wanted to have sex with him at work.

There was no way, absolutely none, that he was going to let Duncan step foot in his showroom ever again. Not after the little show he put on for everyone on that fateful Saturday night dinner.

Not quite ready to take responsibility and own up to his actions, he still held Duncan accountable, not only for the affair, but for getting caught and turning up at his house unannounced. A lot of Daniel's problems could have been prevented if Duncan hadn't turned up out of the blue like that. And who knows, even after sleeping with Billy, Daniel may have been able to win James back, had it not been for him finding out about the affair.

Daniel had never found out that it was Billy that had dropped off the parcel, or that it could easily have been Billy *and* his son catching him in the act. The fear of the unknown had prompted his vow to be more careful in the future. Daniel might have loved no-strings sex, but he respected his business even more. After witnessing the demise of Aiken's, he was more determined than ever to keep his head down and maintain his respectable reputation as both a brand and as a businessman.

Daniel didn't care what could or would fall out from Duncan's immediate termination: tribunals, threats, blackmailing, whatever Duncan could think of doing, Daniel would vehemently fight it any way he needed to. James had already found out, so what else was there to be afraid of?

Instead of waiting to see what Duncan might do though, Daniel needed to be proactive. Going on the offensive, he hoped that he could warn Duncan off from making a bad situation worse all around.

Duncan was young. He wasn't earning great money, and he didn't have immediate family or a mortgage to support. A good looking (albeit rather psychotic) guy like that would find a new job straight away, especially as he was a quick learner and actually very good at what he did.

So, instead of waiting to see if Duncan was going to cause trouble or not, Daniel sent an officially worded email with the intention of putting the issue to bed once and for all:

"Dear Mr Ferguson,

Please take this email as confirmation of the ter-

mination of your contract with Coben Oak, with immediate effect.

Unfortunately, under the circumstances, it is felt that the safest option would be for you not to return to work on Monday, 19th July. I will ensure that any possessions you may have left in the shop are posted to your home address in due course.

I have evidence of you sending unsolicited, sexually explicit images to my home address. I also have several witnesses to corroborate that you have been stalking me and on one occasion you entered my home uninvited, where you became angry and violent towards myself, my husband and my guests.

I will have no choice but to contact the police should you try and return to work on Monday, or threaten me in any way with regards to this situation.

I thank you for your time at Coben Oak, and wish you well in your future endeavours. Under the terms of your contract, and under the difficult situation laid out above, I will ensure that you receive one month's pay in addition to the hours you have worked this month under the condition that you will not contact Coben Oak again, or discuss this issue with any other party.

Regards,

Daniel Coben
Coben Oak."

Fortunately, the letter seemed to do the trick, and at least one of Daniel's problems was quickly resolved. Duncan had taken the extra month's salary and hadn't been heard from again.

Having apparently learnt from past mistakes, Duncan's replacement was a very capable middle-aged woman called Liz. She wasn't interested or capable of helping out in the workshop like Duncan was, but was fantastic on the shop floor with customers. The time Daniel had saved by not teaching, flirting with or shagging her was better spent on working and therefore Daniel's bottom line hadn't suffered.

Liz could be a little bossy on the shop floor. On more than one occasion she'd told him off for looking scruffy when there were customers browsing, but in honestly Daniel liked her sense of pride and ability to manage the showroom. She was proactive with marketing, and had arranged a double page spread in one of the trendy local magazines, which had helped business immensely. Liz made him take regular breaks and did her best to make sure he left on time, which somehow made him more productive, rather than less. All in all, she was doing a great job of managing him and *Coben Oak*.

On a more personal topic, unfortunately, even months after Daniel had found out about James and Billy's budding new relationship, he was still unable to concede and admit his marriage was over. He had sent flowers, chocolates, offers of expensive holidays and more children, but nothing worked. He'd always known that James wouldn't be bought like that, but felt that he had to try, regardless.

He didn't know what else to do. He'd never been the 'chaser' before and he didn't like it, but he really wanted his husband back

Daniel's main problem was that he just couldn't get James to acknowledge that he had changed. He'd promised him there would be no more cheating. No more sly digs at James' appearance, his weight or his thinning hairline. But nothing worked, and for that, he surprised even himself in how sorry he was and what a huge fucking mistake he'd made out of the whole thing. Although he had enjoyed the ride, he'd never envisaged it ruining what he'd had with James.

In retrospect, it seemed a shame that Billy's threat to Kirk had been as successful as it was because in many ways, Daniel and Kirk would have made the most narcissistic couple; perfect for each other in every way. If only Kirk had managed to proposition his ex as he'd intended to then things might have ended up far differently than they had...

James

That fateful Saturday was always going to be a difficult night for James. For all of them, really. There were many reasons, and both he and Billy had expected fireworks one way or another. And one way or another, they got them.

But to see his best friend stabbed like that, even if it had been accidental, was far worse than he could ever have imagined. A thousand times more painful than the triviality of a cheating husband's lover bursting in, or his own affair being exposed in front of everyone.

At least the ambulance came promptly. It seems wrong somehow, even now, to say that they were fortunate enough to have Shirley waiting and watching outside like that. The nosey neighbour that always gave them a hard time, but it was true. No matter how much they loathed her (which wasn't a patch on how she'd felt about them), she was there exactly when they needed her the most.

None of the friends were in the right state of mind to call 999 in those first critical moments. All four of them were in shock. Strangely, not one of them even thought to reach for their phone. Frozen like deer in headlights, panic had set in and they just didn't think to phone for help.

But Shirley, with her perpetual complaining and her over-reacting, for once was the saving grace of the evening. For once, the 999 call she'd placed about them was warranted and greatly appreciated.

True to form, she'd stayed on the street to watch the whole commotion unfold. Doing her duty, she'd informed all of the neighbours and passer-by's that had come out or stopped by to see what was going on. Retreating to her own doorstep as not to appear any nosier than she had to, Shirley was still stood watching by the time the ambulance had closed its doors and was on its way down the street.

The flashing lights had pulled up before Billy lost consciousness. The paramedics were fantastic. Clearly, he'd lost an awful lot of blood – the tablecloth was testament to that. The three friends may not have been explicitly warned to say their goodbyes for the final time, but it was certainly implied by the reaction of the ambulance crew. As they were ushered out of the dining room so the paramedics could do their job, James had overheard one of them saying, 'Jesus, this is bad."

James couldn't believe it. He'd finally fallen for the real love of his life and after only a few short days living together as though they were married, it would all be taken away from him. His 'happy ending' was fleeting and tragic. Not only would he lose his new lover, but his best friend, too. All in one cruel act of confusion.

With all their previous problems brushed to one side for the time being, all three of them travelled to the hospital to be with Billy. James sat with Aiken in the back of the ambulance, whereas Daniel followed closely behind in a taxi.

They'd unanimously agreed, knowing they would have had Billy's blessing, that it had been a tragic accident. It *had* been an accident. Aiken had never intended to kill his husband. That was obvious to all of them.

He was just at his wit's end and had momentarily and foolishly made a snap decision to end his own life. He never meant to hurt anyone else. That too was apparent.

It had all got out of hand for Aiken, and in that split moment, intoxicated by the wine he so rarely binged on, there seemed to be little other option available to him.

They rode in silence for most of the way. Too afraid to talk. Too afraid to actually say their goodbyes.

Closing his eyes for the last time, Billy told Aiken he loved him.

James sat with them, not once feeling like a third wheel. In floods of tears, he stroked Billy's hand before giving Aiken the comforting embrace he desperately needed.

...And Finally

An age had passed since that group of unlikely friends had seen one another altogether. Finally, on a late summer's evening, they had managed to arrange a catch-up meal. Saturday night dinner, just for old time's sake. It certainly wasn't like before, but it would be nostalgic; healing even, none the less.

That evening had been a very close call. It had taken a four-hour battle in the emergency room to try and stabilise Billy. He had needed one of the largest blood transfusions the hospital had ever seen. Twice the surgeon had lost him. The computer screens flatlined, with the telltale drone of a stilled heart on the monitor. But he was a fighter. And now Billy had so much to fight for, it seemed he just wouldn't give up. After such an eventful and life-changing week, who would?

Three weeks after being rushed into the emergency room as close to death as he was, Billy was finally strong enough to return home. *To James and Cleo.*

That fateful dinner was nothing but a distant memory now. Since then, James and Billy had made it official and had been happily married for nearly four years. James had gone back to work, and they had subsequently completed their family with a little daughter of their own named Molly. Neither one of them wished for anything more.

Aiken was now working for Broderick, under the company name *Flowers by Stead*. He was happy not to have the stresses associated with running his own business, but still loved doing what he did every day. With his career back on track again after successfully overcoming his gambling addiction, he had recently begun to date. He was still working on his relationship skills, yet his new partner Jessie was very patient with him. Being the really nice guy that he was, Jessie had brought the best out of Aiken and was a welcome, if not rather unorthodox addition to the evening's dynamic.

Since the incident, for which Billy had never blamed Aiken, the two men had eventually become better friends than they had been in their final years of marriage. It seemed that once the need for a sexual relationship between them had dissipated, there was no reason not to start liking each other again. There was a reason they had fallen in love in the first place, and that reason was still there deep down. They didn't live in each other's pockets, but it was nice every now and again to check in with one another.

Knowing Aiken was a difficult one to crack, Billy had been relieved to hear that he'd found someone willing to give him another chance. He deserved it more than anyone Billy knew.

Tonight was the first time the rest of them had met Jessie,

and Billy couldn't help smile at the sight of his ex-husband. He seemed happy; really, genuinely happy, and Billy was filled with a reassuring warmth. Aiken deserved all of the happiness in the world, and it was no one's fault that that happiness didn't or couldn't come from Billy.

Now that James and Billy were living their happy-ever-afters, and Aiken too was on the right path, that only left Daniel.

Daniel, unlike the rest of them, was exactly the same as he had always been. Arrogant, overworked and over-sexed, but somehow still a little loveable, regrettably.

Between handovers and drop-offs with Cleo, and from what James had head through the grapevine, his ex-husband currently had a string of casual boyfriends that would last no longer than a few months at most. All of them were far younger than him, and it was starting to look a tad obvious. Now forty, Daniel was just starting to show a little tiredness around the eyes, and often felt the lag when trying to keep up with so many younger guys... especially in the bedroom.

Aiken, Billy nor James had anything in common with Daniel that was really worth salvaging. It had always been about his marriage to James that had firmly cemented him in the group. There was one huge exception though, and that was Cleo. For his sake, all three parents were *now* perfectly pleasant to one another, and comfortable in each other's company. Just as they always had been.

It seemed rather fitting therefore, that Daniel had accepted their invitation this evening. Somehow it felt like they had all come full circle.

Tonight, unfortunately, as none of Daniel's usual fuck buddies were available, he joined James and Billy, Aiken and Jessie without the emotional support of a plus one.

Although he'd never admit it, James wondered if he was maybe working on himself, just a little bit, too?

It had been a shame though, because James really wanted to see for himself the mismatch between Daniel and a much younger, hotter, fitter, vibrant boyfriend. Just for old time's sake.

It was their first Saturday night dinner together in the history of them being friends that no one argued, no one bickered and no one ended up drinking too much.

They all had a surprisingly enjoyable evening and promised they would do it again soon.

<u>Acknowledgements</u>

Thank you once again to Tristan, for putting up with me whilst I write. Thank you also for your patience and initial help with the book.

To Bradly Brady, thank you for your encouragement, support and advice. I appreciate the kind words, especially from an author whose work I enjoy so much.

To Andrew May and Spectrum Books, thanks again for your time, effort and interest in my work.

And finally, to all of the friends that have shared Saturday night dinners with Tristan and myself. We've always had fun, and here's to many more.

About the Author

J S Gray was born in the North East of England. After graduating from the university of Huddersfield with a degree in Fine Art, he moved to the picturesque island of Jersey, where he began to write. He lives with his husband and son.

J S Gray published his first novel, *Standing in the Shadows* under the pen name Jon Stasiak, and has recently released a second horror, *Death by a Thousand Cuts.* Confessions of an Art Student was his first LGBTQ novel published in 2020. He has since devoted his time to writing novels which focus on characters under the LGBTQ spectrum, pulling from his own personal experiences. In addition to writing, J S Gray loves painting, photography and spending time with his friends and family.

Excellent LGBTQ+ fiction by unique, wonderful authors.
Thrillers
Mystery
Romance
Young Adult
& More

Join our mailing list here for news, offers and free books!

Visit our website for more Spectrum Books
www.spectrum-books.com

Or find us on Instagram
@spectrumbookpublisher

www.ingramcontent.com/pod-product-compliance
Lightning Source LLC
Chambersburg PA
CBHW021248170626
46808CB00013BA/157